I Should Be So Lucky

BY

LIAM LIVINGS

Beaten Track
www.beatentrackpublishing.com

I Should Be So Lucky

First published 2018 by Beaten Track Publishing
Copyright © 2018 Liam Livings

ISBN: 978 1 78645 268 9

Cover Design: Roe Horvat

Beaten Track Publishing,
Burscough, Lancashire.
www.beatentrackpublishing.com

DEDICATION & ACKNOWLEDGEMENTS

Thanks to Deb for helping make this story really sparkle by working with me and giving it a damned good edit. Thanks also to her for helping bring this story to the world. I'm a new author to the Beaten Track Publishing stable, and it was lovely to join this family.

I need to thank Becky Black and Anna Martin for introducing me to the concept of NaNoWriMo (National Novel Writing Month), without which this book would almost definitely not exist. I respond well to a deadline, you see. *I Should Be So Lucky* was my November 2015 NaNoWriMo novel. I wrote a very rough, very crappy first draft (because honestly, all a first draft has to do is exist as it's only for the author) in fifteen days! At the time, I'd just started my MA in Creative Writing and had plenty enough to do, thank you very much.

I'd like to thank Roe Horvat who has created a perfect cover that shows the heroes, and the sort of glittery, happy, sparkly emotionally uplifting story this is.

I also want to thank my dear departed great auntie, who has provided inspiration for Olive in the story. Great Auntie used to be a cook in a large stately home in Essex. My granddad's acceptance of me as I grew up, combined with Great Auntie's deadpan responses to life's trials and tribulations were very useful when writing this book.

Almost done now—I want to thank my favourite 'Princess of Pop' for creating and performing fabulous, sparkly, emotional, uplifting, catchy songs for over thirty years. You know who I mean. ;-)

Finally, I want to thank you, dear reader. I hope this book gives you as much pleasure as my favourite songs from my 'Princess of Pop'. If it does, then I really should be so lucky!

Love and light,

Liam Livings xx

I Should Be So Lucky

CHAPTER 1

Julian

AFTER OUR PERFORMANCE at Wembley Arena, there was, as usual, a party in Soho at one of the clubs you access through a hidden door round the back of a shop and down some stairs. One of the other dancers bought the first round, and I took my turn buying the celebratory vodka and Cokes; one of the guys was celebrating getting a new job supporting acts on a TV talent show. I thought it was a step down, but he was made up, so who was I to burst his bubble? Then there was a taxi whisking us to a club in Vauxhall with me and the other gay male dancers…and that was where I met someone.

"What do you do?" he asked, his large pupils scanning me slowly while he chewed his cheek.

"I'm a backing dancer for Sallie." She's one of those famous people who only needs to use her first name and everyone knows who you mean.

His eyes lit up. "Sallie? As in *the Sallie*? Used to be in that Australian soap as the tomboy carpenter in the eighties, Sallie?"

Suddenly his too-butch-to-be-gay act came tumbling down around his ears, as I'd suspected it would. He didn't look as straight-acting as he had minutes before, a mass of sexual tension and hormones and manliness. Now, he was clapping and squealing excitedly about my Australian Pop Princess boss and whether I could get him backstage tickets.

"Maybe," I replied, eyeing up the empty glass on the shiny metal bar. "Get me another drink and we'll see."

He bought me another drink, and another, and another, and before long we'd kissed a few times and moved on from Sallie talk to other stuff, like how far his place was and if I wanted to come back with him.

The last bit was said with a raised eyebrow and a leering curl of his lips.

Bored of the thumping music, and with all the inevitability of Wednesday following Tuesday, I went home with him.

I won't go into the details of the sex because it was pretty standard. When you have as much as I do, with as many different men as I do, it all becomes a bit of a blur. Not that I don't enjoy it; I do, otherwise I wouldn't do it. And I'm game for anything; I'll give anything a go at least once—as long as it's legal—and I always take care of myself. I'm not stupid.

I'd give it a six or seven, if I had to pick. Yeah, a six or seven I'd give it. *Him*, I mean. I'm a good eight or nine, darling. Of course I am.

Afterwards, he asked—I don't remember his name, he may not have told me, I don't remember telling him mine—while wiping the stickiness off his smooth chest, "What time you thinking of leaving?"

I took a quick glance around his bedroom—all chrome and black wood, mirrored wardrobes and nothing on display. Reminded me of a luxury car showroom. "I could go now, to be honest." I shrugged.

"Whatever. If you want," he replied, moving closer to me on the bed.

I braced myself. *Is he going to be a hugger?* I knew I couldn't cope with another hugger. There'd been a succession of those last year. Given the option of a hugger and a fuck-and-goer, I'd always pick the latter.

He spooned me from behind and put his arms around my waist, kissing my back, stroking my navel with his fingers. "If you don't have to rush off, stay. We can cuddle."

I removed his hands from my waist, jumped from the bed and pulled my trousers and T-shirt on in a few quick movements. My underwear had been ripped off and used earlier, so I thought it best to let crusty Calvin's lie on the floor. "Bye." I was at the bedroom door now, waving.

He knelt on the bed, his cock and balls squeezed between his legs, nestling among stubble where he'd shaved *down there*. It was slightly hilarious, slightly ridiculous and not in the least bit sexy.

"See you, then," I said.

"Do you want my number?"

I inwardly sighed. A cuddler and a can-I-have-your-number-er too. *I'm definitely best off out of this one.* I smiled as he scribbled his number on a bit of paper and handed it to me. I put it in my pocket.

"What about yours?"

"I'll text you, then you'll have mine."

"We could do coffee in Soho. Go to see that Sallie exhibition you said was on at the V&A museum…"

I didn't hear the rest because I was now in the cool early morning air, on the pavement outside his house, thanking my lucky stars I'd got out of there with my sanity intact, and wondering how long it would take to get back to my place in Paddington.

***

A few hours later, I woke in my bed. My own glorious bed, in my own glorious bedroom, in my own glorious flat that I shared with Angie, who was pretty glorious in her own way too. No bunny-boiler boyfriends in the making, kneeling on the bed and asking me to date them.

I threw on the red and gold silk kimono I'd picked up in Japan during the last Sallie tour and shuffled slowly downstairs to the kitchen.

Angie sat at the kitchen table smoking menthol cigarettes, her brown hair tied back in a bun and her face covered in white make-up like a Geisha girl. "What time did you get in?"

I sat at the table and pushed my coffee mug next to the three-quarters-full cafetière. "Be gentle with me."

"Sore, are you?" She filled my mug with strong black coffee and added four large spoons of sugar.

"Because no, I'm not sweet enough."

We laughed at our ongoing joke about my sugar addiction.

"What do you want this time? I'm long haul to Australia, via Dubai, so anything I can get you?"

"Ralph Lauren eau de toilette, the green bottle, not the orange one. That smelt of cat piss. Chucked it down the toilet."

"Sorry it wasn't up to His Royal Highness's standards." She was making a note on her phone.

I shifted from one bum cheek to the other on the chair, then took a big gulp of coffee.

"Sore head?"

"And the rest. We finished, then he asked when I was leaving. I'd have stayed awhile, actually, but then he got all clingy and boyfriendy. Couldn't get out of there fast enough."

"Where *do* you meet these people?"

"Never mind that, why do they think a fuck in a club is going to turn into a boyfriend? If I wanted a boyfriend, I wouldn't be in Vauxhall at five a.m. talking to someone who'd certainly had more than a few gin and tonics."

Angie shook her head. "Eau de toilette. Anything else?"

"Some phone bits. They're dirt cheap in the Middle East, aren't they?"

She shook her head.

"And some of that designer luggage."

"You still owe me for the Gucci carry-on and man-bag I bought you."

"Add it to the list. Put it on the fridge door. I'll transfer the money when I get paid." Or next month. "I turned up to the last tour and three other dancers had the same luggage. Not similar, but exactly the fucking same. Same colour, size, brand—everything. Mortified! I almost bin-bagged it there and then, but I wouldn't have had anywhere to hold my stuff." I tutted loudly.

"Your shallowness knows no bounds."

I finished giving her my order of goods, and we talked about when she'd be back.

"A week. Two-day stop-over in Sydney, and then I'm back again. So you've got the place to yourself. And please, if you have a party or invite any trade round, can you make sure you clean up afterwards? I never got that stain out of the cushion."

"Sorry." I blushed at the memory of how the cushion had become stained. I'd only just got rid of the six-foot-six rugby-playing 'straight' man—the reason for the stain—fifteen minutes before Angie had returned home.

"Fancy some breakfast? Bacon and eggs?"

I glanced at the empty mug of coffee. "What do you think this is? Scotch mist?"

"Nice thick slices of bacon, and a snotty egg, covered in ketchup and slices of toast on the side."

I retched slightly at the thought, then held my mug in the air. "Please."

Angie filled my mug then hers and asked, "That's the third one this month. Why do you think there are so many guys like that?"

"I think they pretend to be fuck-and-go, but really they want cuddles and a takeaway on the sofa. There's not an app for that. It could be called Cudlr, or something."

"You're not tempted by a bit of cuddling and sofa action?"

"Not at the moment. Why would I?"

"Someone to have a laugh with, get old with, to snuggle up with."

"I've got friends for that. Why do people think you have to get everything you need in one person? What's wrong with splitting it? Some people for sex, and others for everything else. Much neater."

We sat in silence for a few moments. Angie smiled and eyed me up slowly, her nose sniffing to the side in a gesture that told me she was far from convinced but that the conversation was now over. "When are you next working?"

"I said be gentle with me. I said I was sore. What's with the third degree?"

"Not today, I take it?"

"What do you think?" I waved at the semi-naked firemen calendar on the wall. "It's on that. Check, would you? I'm too weak to stand." I fluttered my eyelashes at her.

"You're such a tart." She walked to the calendar, peering at it closely, then said, "Nothing for over a week. Lucky you."

"Maybe I'll meet my own fireman." We often talked about my penchant for men in uniform, and in particular the rescue services—fire, ambulance, police. I'd developed it after once pulling a Westminster Council parking attendant who'd tried to give me a ticket in Soho Square until I'd charmed my way out of it, and him into the back of my car. Unfortunately, the allure of an electronic penalty-charge machine was nothing compared with a policeman's helmet or a fireman's hose.

But a wank in the car is worth two parking tickets on the dashboard, isn't it?

CHAPTER 2

Troy

A RE YOU WITH me or not?" Freya shouted at me as she stood with her hands on her hips in our kitchen.

"I don't know what you want from me. I live here. We've been together for seven years. I dug you the pond you wanted in the garden. What more can I do?"

"I want more than a pond. Which, by the way, you've only half dug. I want commitment. I want you to *show* me you're serious about *us*."

Always the emphasis on the word, *us*. Always at the end of the sentence, accompanied with a stare. *Us.*

"Seven years and no wedding. No proposal. And kids? There's no chance. Every time I mention them you leave the room. Might as well be talking about booking a holiday to the Moon for all the likelihood of us having kids."

"I want to do it at the right time, babes. I don't want to rush into it. I want to give the kid a proper life."

"First time you've said that much about it. I'll come off the pill, I said. But every time you're in with the condoms. It's not like I've got anything infectious. I've only been with you for the last seven years. But no, every time, even though I'm still on the pill you pop on a hat."

"Double Dutch method it's called." *And the just in case method, I call it.* The thought of kids was interesting, like the thought of climbing Mount Everest—something I stood back in

7

awe when others did but not something I really wanted to happen in my life.

"I know what it's called. What I want to know is why we're still doing it when we could be having a family."

"When the time is right."

"I'm thirty-fucking-three. My biological clock is ticking so loud it wakes me in the morning like an alarm clock."

Am I being selfish not really wanting kids and not actually telling her? I'd had this conversation with some of my football friends with kids. For them, it seemed it was definitely a joint decision; they had both wanted to start a family. It wasn't like going on a holiday you didn't want, or to a concert to see an act you didn't like. Having a child was a lifetime decision.

Staring at my hands, I said, "I don't know what I want."

Freya shouted, "Well, it's taken you fucking long enough to make a decision. Are you with me or not? I'm sick and tired of all this titting around. I love you, and I want to start a family with you. What's so complicated about that?"

"Nothing."

"And so?" She stared at me, her voice quieter now, her smile... the same smile that had enchanted me when we first met.

"I don't know."

"Don't know what? If you love me, or if you want to have a family together? *Us.*"

I did love her. I cared a great deal about her. I would never wish any harm on her. And we'd had some great times together, great memories of our relationship—holidays, silly in-jokes we'd shared—and her family were like a second family to me. But, even now, after seven years, there was still this nagging feeling about something missing in our relationship, and it wasn't children.

I said, barely audible now, avoiding her eyes, "I'm wasting your time. Probably best I go."

"Go forever, or for tonight? What do you mean, go?" She hugged me, squeezing my bum just like on our first date when I'd hoped against all evidence to the contrary that things would last this time. Only now, I was still in the same place, and it wasn't fair to her to continue stringing her along.

"I love you, and that's why I'm going. Find yourself another man who knows he wants to have kids. I don't know if I want to have kids, which I think says it all." I removed her hands from my body and walked to the front door.

Freya ran after me. She stood in the hall, her fists bunched at her sides and her face red. "Don't worry about the fucking pond. It doesn't matter. I love you. You can't leave. What about *us*?"

"That's why I'm leaving." I closed the door behind me and drove to the only place I could think of: Finchingfield Abbey where I worked as a groundsman.

***

I was eleven when I realised I was a bit different from many other boys my age, and I already knew it wasn't a good thing. I saw other boys who couldn't play sport and stood, with rain-covered glasses, waiting to be picked for a team. We used to laugh at boys like that for being different. Different wasn't something I wanted to be.

***

Finchingfield Abbey was a large stately home in Essex, near the Suffolk border, on the edge of the chocolate-box village of Finchingfield. It had a village green, windmill and guildhall which was the village's beating heart, containing the library, shop and museum. The abbey and my work there had always been somewhere to escape disagreements with Freya, and Olive—the cook—was always there for some down-to-earth advice and a sympathetic ear.

Dumping my bag on the stone kitchen floor, I asked Olive if I could stay for a while.

She removed her blue hair net, combed her short white hair through her hands and sat at the large pine table in the middle of the room. Her cheeks were permanently flushed from standing over the Aga for twenty years. "What the bleedin' 'ell have you been and gone and done now?"

"Nothing. I just need somewhere to stay for a bit. I'll set up one of the staff bedrooms."

"They're all for storage. Full of the antiques the family need to sell to run this place. Even I don't live in now."

"Ah. Not to worry, I'll sleep in the car. Flatten the seats down, I'll be fine. You haven't got a blanket I could borrow, have you?"

"What are we gonna do with you, eh? Tell me what's gone on and we'll clear one of the rooms for you. But only a few nights, mind. If the family finds out, we'll both be out on our ears."

I followed Olive along a narrow corridor off the kitchen, and up a few flights of stairs to a long corridor with a series of doors off it. The nearest one opened to a small room with a single bed, a sink and a wardrobe. The floor was covered in packets of flour and sugar and tins of food.

"Home sweet home," Olive said. "You get the tins, I'll shift the flour, and you can tell me what's gone on."

As we cleared the room, moving its contents to the next staff bedroom, piling the food among the antiques, I told her what had happened.

She listened without question until we'd cleared the room, then she sat on the squeaky, single, metal-framed bed. "When you started 'ere seven years ago, hadn't you just split from someone then?"

"Penny."

"That's the one. Wanted kids, didn't she?"

"And the rest. Wedding, two-point-four children, car on hire purchase, new kitchen, three-piece suite every three years." I shook my head.

"Hate to say it, love, but you're not getting any younger. This is the sort of thing I'd expect from one of my kitchen girls, or that young lad who fixes all the household cars, not someone in his for'ies."

I shrugged, because there was nothing else to be said about that.

"Thought you loved her."

"I do. That's why I left."

Olive patted the bed next to her, asked me to sit and tell her what was really the matter.

I repeated what I'd already told her, but said nothing about the something missing.

After a while, she threw me a blanket and told me to be quiet—she'd see me in the morning if I fancied a cooked breakfast. "Go to work on an egg, they used to say in the war. It'll all look better in the morning after a good night's kip."

***

Dear Dave—

I had named my diary because it felt less poncey than writing 'Dear Diary'.

—history repeated itself. It's over with Freya. I don't feel like it was bound to happen, but at the end, during the argument, it was the only thing that could happen. Another seven years. What is it with me and the seven-year itch? Why don't these relationships stick? I thought it was all going along nicely, and suddenly we're shouting about half-dug ponds, and kids and weddings, and I knew it wasn't for me.

11

All I've ever done was go along with what she wanted—no questions, no disagreements with Freya. Whatever she asked for, I got it for her. I didn't realise a family was so important to her. She said she'd told me, but I don't remember. I definitely loved her—still love her, but there's something missing.

Just wish I knew what the hell it was.

CHAPTER 3

Julian

I ARRIVED EARLY AT the O2 Arena because Sallie had invited all the backstage and onstage members of the company for drinks. 'Me and my boys', she liked to call it. It was mainly a male onstage crew; Sallie's act worked better with male dancers since most of her fans were gay men and straight women.

And yes, if I'm being one hundred percent honest, I had slept with some of the other male dancers. One of them, Bjorn, was still my go-to at the end of the night if we'd both failed to pick up someone new. 'It's only sex' we had both agreed numerous times. The first time Bjorn came over to my place to talk pensions—I had a private one, and he needed someone to talk him through the basics because he didn't understand them—we ended up in bed together, and it had continued from there.

Now, I was backstage, watching the warm-up act—some girl group trying to sing live and failing miserably. Meow.

Familiar hands reached around my waist, and a pair of equally familiar lips planted a kiss on my neck. I turned to kiss him back.

Bjorn—blond, Swedish, full of Viking genes, square-jawed and bulging with muscles, with a wide grin—kissed me back. "Nervous?"

"First night of Sallie's biggest tour in ten years, us on for every costume change and no understudies? Piece of piss."

He laughed.

***

The opening of the concert involved Bjorn and I carrying Sallie—sitting on a gold throne and wearing a crown and an ermine cape—on stage. She started by singing one of her cheesy eighties hits. Naturally, the whole audience knew every word and sang along.

Bjorn and I stood either side and copied her dance moves until the final bars of the song when we lifted her back onto the throne and carried her off stage for the first of sixteen costume changes of the evening.

The concert passed well; the audience sang along to the classics and cheered at the new songs. For Bjorn's and my next big number, we stood either side of a bath filled with bubbles into which we lowered Sallie. She wore a pink bikini and shower cap while Bjorn and I were bare-chested, a short pink towel wrapped around our waists and cartoon-style pink plastic hair over our real hair, giving the appearance of cartoon-character heads on male model torsos. It was exactly the sort of mixing it up and shameless appealing to gay men that Sallie did so often and so well. The song she sang was about her being the most fortunate girl in the world, and how fate had simply come into her life. It was a classic bubble-gum-pop song from the eighties, and the audience loved it. They cheered at the start, sang along with the chorus and begged for more when it ended.

Sallie then climbed into a golden trapeze seat suspended above the audience, swinging from side to side of the arena, sometimes a few feet above the audience's heads and at other times near the ceiling. She wore a black feathered dress with a hat in the shape of a crow's head while singing about love birds and how love songs didn't always make sense when they got together. The audience, almost all gay men, lit their cigarette lighters and waved them in the air in time with the music.

With a nod to the techie guys backstage, she raised the tempo a few beats, and the backing track of one of her disco number ones began to play. Enormous glittering disco balls were lowered from the lighting rig to appear either side of the stage. When I'd watched the rehearsal, it had reminded me of one thing and one thing only, to which Bjorn had said, "You have a one-track mind. I like. The audience will not see it this way."

Currently on our sixth costume change of the evening, Bjorn and I wore tiny silver glittering shorts—hot pants for men, basically—with matching shoes. As you can probably imagine, it was one of my favourite parts of the concert and one on which I'd lingered during rehearsals.

The audience sang and waved along to the music, the tension rising as we danced towards the extravagant finale.

CHAPTER 4

Troy

I STOOD BACKSTAGE AT the Sallie concert at the O2 Arena. Having been at the casualties area at the last concert—which had got pretty messy, people with eyes rolled into the back of their heads, tongues hanging out and babbling nonsense—this time I had asked my St John Ambulance boss if I could be backstage first aid. From where I stood, I could see the two backing dancers' outfits— little silver shorts and sparkly shoes. The shorts were very tight and didn't leave much to the imagination. The men filled them well, with large bulges on them both. I shook that thought away and returned to watching Sallie in her black feathered outfit. The audience was mainly gay men, some holding hands, some with beards, some with spiky hair. Most looked like any other man, except for when they kissed the bloke next to them.

Fascinated by what I saw, my gaze drifted back to the dancers. Both obviously worked out at the gym; their bodies had sculpted lines running in a V from their hips to their groins, beneath the towels. Their pecs were what could only be described as chiselled, and the hair was trimmed and covered in a sprinkling of glitter— it was a Sallie concert after all. Their bodies were different from mine—gym bodies as opposed to a hard-labour-outside-in-the-garden body. I wondered how often they went worked out to keep in shape. My stomach tightened, realising I'd been staring at the men's chests for most of the song.

As Sallie reached the end of the number, the glitter balls retracted upwards, disappearing into the lighting rig, or one did.

The other seemed to stick and shook violently. Someone cried out. Then the audience screamed. Before I knew what was happening, the glitter ball hurtled from the ceiling and landed on one of the dancers.

Shit! This is where I come in. This is my moment. This is why I'm here!

I ran on stage carrying my first-aid kit and crouched next to the dancer. The glitter ball was a few feet away and thankfully hadn't broken. It was presumably made of some sort of hard plastic and had bounced slightly on the stage before rolling a few feet away.

"What's his name?" I shouted to Sallie and the other dancer.

Sallie replied, "Julian."

I crouched close to his face, briefly noticing his distinctive eau de toilette and body smell. "Julian, can you hear me? My name's Troy. I'm a trained St John Ambulance volunteer and I'm going to look after you."

Julian rubbed his head and stared at me, his eyes spinning around slightly. "Don't mind me, the show must go on. The fans have come to see Sallie. And I've gone and..." He passed out.

I checked his breathing, which luckily was normal. I noticed he had long brown eyelashes and full lips. I quickly reminded myself of the first-aid checks I needed to complete and was relieved his pulse was also within the normal range.

Sallie put her hand on my arm. "Will he be right? Can I go on?"

"He'll be fine."

"Sure?"

I nodded. "Normal speech, normal vital signs. I'm sure." As gently as I could, I hoisted Julian over my shoulder in a fireman's lift and carried him off stage.

As we reached the wings, he said into my ear, "The show must go on."

I carried him to the treatment area and laid him on a bed, covered him with a blanket and hooked him up to a machine to measure his blood pressure, heart beat and temperature.

Sallie's voice filled the room announcing the dancer would be fine before she continued with the next song.

"What's your name?" I felt his head, where a large bump had already formed.

"Julian." He put his hand on mine as I continued feeling his head for injuries.

"How many fingers am I holding up?" I held three fingers a few inches from his face.

"Three."

After establishing he didn't feel sick or dizzy and didn't have any blurry vision, I explained I'd need to get a nurse to check more formally.

"Aren't you a nurse?" he asked, finishing with an enchanting smile.

"St John Ambulance. First aid." I smiled back at him, my heart beating a little faster than normal.

"Don't mind me."

As we waited for the nurse to respond to my walkie-talkie call, the awkwardness I felt staring at a man wearing only a towel three feet away from me on a bed was soon replaced with Julian's nineteen-to-the-dozen chatter.

He told me how he became a Sallie backing dancer—"Italia Conti school, *Top of The Pops*, standing in for a girl band, then, because I'd been sleeping with the choreographer, dancing for Sallie"—he paused, looking me up and down in my St John Ambulance green uniform. "Nice epaulettes. Very butch." He gave me another blast of that smile.

My heart did a little flutter that it didn't have any right to do, especially since I was only just out of a relationship. Poor Freya. But there was something about Julian; not just his body, which, now I'd had a long close look at it, was pretty spectacular—

from an admiration of another man's hard work point of view, nothing more. There was also his smile, his laugh, the way he listened when I told him about how I had got into the St John Ambulance—"Volunteering, wanting to do a different sort of job from gardening. Gives me a chance to meet a lot of different people and see events all over."

Julian adjusted his position, pulling the towel down to cover himself more. "Yes I am, in case you were wondering."

"What?" I'd had trouble keeping up with his banter, but this was way over my head.

"Am I wearing anything under the towel? Yes. Imagine if it fell down on stage." He giggled, blinking slowly with those long brown eyelashes I'd stared at a bit too long.

My heart was beating faster. My mouth was dry. Before I could work out what that was about, Dolores the nurse arrived in a bustle of "How are you?" and "Has he been looking after you?" and "Let's see what your head's like." She soon decided Julian could be taken somewhere else and didn't need to be under observation any longer. "You all right to take him?" she asked.

"Just to make sure he's steady on his feet." I caught the nurse's eye as I grabbed Julian's hand, put his arm over my shoulder and led him to the dressing room. He limped and winced with pain.

When we reached the dressing room, I walked him to a chair and lowered him gently into it. "I think I should sit with you, just for a bit. Make sure you're OK. I wouldn't want to leave you for you to pass out again and fall off the chair."

"My very own fireman rescuing me."

"St John Ambulance volunteer."

He laughed at my correction. "You've heard about me, tell me about you. I'll ask questions to take my mind off the pain in my leg."

I repeated what I'd said about volunteering for the St John Ambulance, why I enjoyed it, what I was hoping to do.

Julian waved his hand. "I know that. I remember that. Tell me about *you*, not your job. You." He grabbed his leg. "This is killing me. Have a look, would you?"

And so, because I didn't know what else to say and the room was empty except for us two, and because he had the sort of face that made people tell their secrets, while I examined his leg I told him about Freya—the end of our relationship, the non-existent babies, the half-finished pond—everything. I finished with, "Your leg may be fractured."

Julian rubbed it. "You're the hero. You're the rescuer. Freya wants her head examining. A fine specimen of a man like you. I wouldn't chuck you out for a half-finished pond." He pulled himself up on his elbows then leant forward and kissed me on the cheek.

Never mind the smell and the smile and the laugh; the kiss gave me an instant boner. It filled me with questions, with panic, and so I did all I could think of doing, and ran out the room without saying anything more.

***

Even though I had these feelings, I couldn't say *I'm gay* to myself, never mind out loud or to anyone else. Those words were something that had nothing to do with me, my life and how I felt. So I held my breath, I kept it pushed deep down inside, telling myself it was the clothes and not the men inside them I was interested in. I held myself in, hid from everyone, never fully relaxing in case I let the thoughts about it come too close to the surface.

CHAPTER 5

Julian

A FEW DAYS LATER, I was on self-prescribed bed rest at home and I'd spun out the *Hunky Fireman Rescues Me* story over three long days of telling Angie.

She arrived in my room with a tray of precious essential things I'd asked her to fetch me. "Flat Lucozade, face mask, and DVD of *An Officer and a Gentleman*, as requested."

"Ange, you are an angel. In fact, I might start calling you that. Angel. It suits you." I sipped the Lucozade and grabbed the film.

Angie perched on the corner of my bed. "It's a good job I love you. And Angel is not happening, or I will be forced to call your mum and she can look after you."

"Understood. No Angel."

From behind her back, she produced the fireman's calendar. "Thought you might like a quick look at this."

"Honestly, Ange, if you'd seen the bulge in his green jumpsuit uniform. And the deep-brown eyes. And the big strong arms. Did I tell you about the big strong arms and how he carried me off stage to the dressing room?"

"Darling, you've not only told me, you've acted it out, written it down and emailed me the full transcript."

"I've got to have something to occupy myself since Sallie's given me three weeks off."

"What I don't understand—what's been niggling at me since you first told me—is why is a straight man one minute all chatty and spending time with you, and next thing he's gone."

"Poof."

"As in gone in a poof?"

"No, he's a poof. Or bisexual." I winked lasciviously.

"That is what I'm thinking."

"What do you mean? He did clear off a bit sharpish at the end—no goodbye, no nice to meet you, nothing. Normally, straight blokes, if they can take the banter and get into the whole flirting thing, they want to see me again. But this one, nothing. Gone, he was, like a thief in the night, or something."

"He told you about the ex-girlfriend," Angie said. "That's vulnerable. That's opening up, is that."

"His big brown eyes were so lost…so sad when he told me about the ex-girlfriend. Bless."

"Do you think you'll hear from him?"

"How? He jumped ship. My kiss was too much…" It was as if I had been carrying a large coin the size of a pizza, and at that point, I dropped it. "Do you think it was the kiss?"

"Up till then he was fine, wasn't he?"

"Banting away like a good'un, spilling his heart, telling me everything. It was like one of those scenes in *Beaches* when they're growing up and they do everything together. Only we were both male, and not American. You get my point."

"I do, and it's somehow made even more gay by the *Beaches* reference." She scanned the room, asked if I had everything I needed, then said she was on a nonstop to LA and had to go. She kissed my cheek and left me in silence.

The kiss started my brain whirring about the kiss with the St John Ambulance man. I stared at 'May' in the hunky fireman calendar, chucked it on the floor and switched to wondering how long I could get away with being off sick before anyone became suspicious.

CHAPTER 6

Troy

DEAR DAVE,

I don't really know what this all means. I met this dancer at a Sallie concert, and we were chatting in the changing room. All normal. Then, when he said goodbye and thanked me, he kissed me on the cheek. I got a boner straight away. His smell was something I hadn't ever noticed before—musky, manly, not like Freya or any women I've been with before. His voice was a bit high, a bit—feminine I suppose you could say, but he was a backing dancer for Sallie— what was I expecting? But he's definitely a man.

I wanted to stay in the changing room with him—Julian, he said his name was. I wanted to stay there talking to him for ever. It was so easy, just chatting and laughing about something and nothing. I had to leave. As soon as I got a boner, I had to get out of there. I didn't know what would have happened next.

I asked at the St John Ambulance if Sallie's doing any more UK concerts, said I'd be happy to volunteer to do their first aid. Just because, well, it was fun. It was a fun evening.

Bought a tour DVD of Sallie—she has loads of tour DVDs—who knew she'd been on tour so many times? I paused it earlier today to find this Julian guy. Wanted to find out his surname so I could do some Facebook research to find him.

Why? Friends…we got on like friends. I've never met a gay guy and clicked so easily. He was just normal. Like any other guy, only he was gay. It was easy. I know this is bordering on stalking, but it's all innocent. Fuck's sake, I used to get a stiffy on the bus to school all the time. I read in GQ magazine, that men think about sex at least ten times a day. Must have been missing physical contact since splitting with Freya—there's only so much wanking I can do. I'd have fucked a toilet roll last night if I'd had time, so someone kissing me is bound to do stuff.

***

I stood at the door of the building. Cook's hospitality had run out, and I'd managed to find myself a room in a house share not far away.

"How's things? Getting settled now?" Olive asked, reaching forward to pinch my cheek. "Eating enough, are you?"

I wanted to tell her how disappointed I was after doing first aid at a Sallie concert at Newmarket race course and not seeing that dancer. Julian. That was his name. But I didn't tell her that. I'm not one hundred percent sure what it means or how I feel about it myself, so I'm not about to go shouting my personal feelings to everyone. Anyone.

Instead, I shuffled my feet on the stone floor and talked about the flower beds and bulbs and how many hours it had taken me today to clear the beds and plant the bulbs ready for the beginning of the open-house season.

Olive said, wiping her hands on her apron, "Fancy something to eat before you go home? I bet a pound to the penny you're living on ready meals at your place."

I had actually been eating cheese and crackers when I got home each evening, and occasionally Pot Noodles if I fancied a change. Freya's cooking wasn't the only thing I missed, though.

"All right." I sat at the kitchen table, resting my hands on the wooden pine and picking my fingers, wanting to ask something but not sure how to say it out loud.

Olive put a steaming bowl of soup and hunk of bread in front of me. "Veg, from the garden you're tending, so it's only right you get a bit. Tuck in, then there's a bit of left over steak and kidney pie if you want."

I nodded. This was the sort of food I'd not eaten in months. Not since leaving Freya, which I didn't regret, not now, but somehow not being with her had given me lots of time—too much time, in fact—to think about things, especially one thing in particular.

"When you turned forty..." I paused, trying to assemble the words in my mind carefully.

"Yes, love. It was a few decades ago, now. But I do remember. You know what the cruellest or the best thing about getting older is?"

"What?" I stuffed my mouth with bread thickly buttered and dipped another hunk into the soup.

"Even though I'm nearly seventy, I don't feel a day different from when I was in my thirties. Not in here." She tapped her head, then turned to the Aga to busy herself with pots and pans.

"When you turned forty, did you notice any changes? Only..." I trailed off, not sure what to say and not wanting to put words into her mouth. I wanted to hear her response without knowing where I was really coming from with my question.

"What like, Troy love?"

I shrugged and pushed my bowl away from me. She removed it and replaced it with a huge plate of pie, mashed potato and veg, covered in gravy.

"My Albie, he went a bit funny when he turned forty. God bless his soul." She crossed herself with her right hand. "He went and bought himself a little sports car, started wearing clothes our sons would have worn, suddenly wanted to get into these new

27

sports he'd not talked about before. Kept saying he wanted to try all these new things."

"And did he?"

"Some of them, he did. Some things stuck. He was friends with a younger man from the local clay pigeon shooting club for a while. Did everything together, they did. The sports car didn't last long—bit of a five-minute wonder really. He found it messed his hair up and gave him back pain on a long drive. And he didn't stop bloody well complaining about the road tax and insurance and petrol bills for another car. Yeah, that soon went."

"What would you say are the signs of a mid-life crisis?" I doubted she'd mention a sudden interest in a dancer of the same gender but thought it was worth asking anyway.

"Albie looked at his life and thought he wanted to do more, to experience new things. It's easy, when you get older, when you get to forty, to get stuck on only doing certain things and not trying anything new."

So nothing about a dancer of my gender then? Shame. I stared at my plate of food and shovelled another forkful into my mouth.

Olive sat next to me, watching me eat. "Stomach think your throat's been cut, eh?"

I nodded, pushing away the thoughts about pausing the Sallie tour DVD and trying to zoom in on the dancer's upper body and face. I was impressed by his gym physique, that's all it was, surely? But the internet loop I'd found myself in after that video, involving muscle pecs and then a long time on a website about men's body hair and the patterns it grew in, were all things afterwards I'd mentally clicked away, like the internet browsers and history—despite it being my own laptop. Now, the thought that lingered—more than the pictures of the men's body hair and the dancer's face—was how I had lobbed another fucking boner that afternoon. Not at the men's body hair pictures—that was a bit funny as some of the poor guys looked more like bears and had all sorts of issues with sweat and shaving rash—but the pictures on the dancer's Facebook page, of him on holiday at the beach, smiling, in a pair of tiny swimming shorts, and another picture of him in a shirt with the top three buttons undone, revealing his chest. Three buttons because I'd counted them, and then saved the picture.

"Want spotted dick and custard? It's got dates and raisins in it, 'cos Her Upstairs wanted it brought up to date, and seen some programme with that saucy celebrity chef woman who's always busting out of her bras and dribbling chocolate sauce over everything."

Spotted dick? Chocolate sauce dribbling over everything? "I best get home." I stood quickly, the chair making a squealing noise on the stone floor.

Even the thought of telling anyone what I was thinking…I was so scared it would ruin everything, and everyone in my world would reject me as it would make me a different person.

CHAPTER 7

Julian

NEVER BEFORE HAS one man made such a little accident into such a big deal, believed by so many gullible gay men, and got himself such a lot of sympathetic cock because of it.

I know, I know, it's a bit immoral, or dishonest, or something with 'un' or 'de' at the start, but come on! Sometimes you've got to work with what life gives you. When life gives you lemons, make lemonade—isn't that what they say? Or something.

Now, let me see, what have I been up to since being off work? Oh yes. Monday, it was the student from some London uni, drama student, obvs, saw me with my stick in the bar.

"Do you want a hand with the drinks?" he'd asked.

He was in his early twenties, and they can go all night in my experience, so I looked a bit winsome and said, "If you don't mind."

There followed a scene where I explained what I did and how I'd come to be in such an unfortunate situation—the fireman, of course, featured in the story. I know he wasn't a fireman, but the student wasn't going to know.

I said, "I'm waiting for a friend, but he's not turned up, so I'll probably just go home." Always works, that one, especially in certain bars, with enough *Poor Me* ladled on for good measure— well, I had a whole cauldron of the stuff and was ladling it on like it was going out of fashion.

"I'm waiting for my friends. Mind if I sit with you for a bit?" He smiled. His hair pointed in about six different directions at the same time. He wore lots of black guyliner and had big hands with silver rings on his thumbs.

Big hands and you know what that means…

A few drinks later, we were laughing and chatting like old friends, only it was clear both of us had one thing in mind.

He grabbed my hand and put it on his thigh where I was pleased to find not just thigh, but a very thick, very far down his thigh semi-erection. "How far can you walk with that stick?"

On the tip of my tongue was *how far can you walk with your big stick*? But I'd been pretty understated to that point—as far as I ever can—so I didn't want to lose the magic, and instead simply said, "Cab would be better."

In the taxi, he unzipped his flies and put my hands inside his underwear. It was all I could do to stop myself getting on my knees and noshing him off. Fuck me, it was magnificent. Sadly, the kneeling on the floor would have blown my *poor invalid* cover. He was cupping my balls and tweaking my nipples under my T-shirt while snogging me, rubbing my face with his stubbly chin and biting my lips.

We arrived at a house off the main road somewhere in South London—could've been Southwark, could've been Bromley, I didn't know and I didn't give a shit.

We fell into the hallway on the floor, He kicked the door shut and shouted some names; I assumed his housemates'. No one replied so he pointed upstairs. He walked behind me, right behind me, his cock pushing onto my bum as we climbed each step. I was making a bit of a meal out of it—dodgy leg, of course.

He pushed me down on the stairs, pulled my jeans and pants off, and after whispering in my ear what he was going to do, only pausing to rubber himself up and spit on his hand, he fucked me there and then on the stairs.

It. Was. Fan-fucking-tastic.

He reached round to my cock while he was drilling in and out of me and pulled on me in the same rhythm.

I gasped because I was so close but wanted to prolong the delicious fullness he gave me with each thrust. Unlike so many big boys, he knew exactly how to use it, teasing me with the tip, then plunging in balls deep before pulling out again, and repeating the whole thrust, all the while wanking me with his hand and kissing my neck.

With a gasp, I came all up the carpet stairs.

"Quick. Shall I?" he whispered into my ear.

"Fuck me," I replied, my voice strangled as I tried to concentrate on forming words while his cock still filled me so perfectly.

It didn't take long until he came, with a long, final thrust deep into my arse and a shiver as he gasped into my neck. He waited there for a few moments, both of us locked together, before he gently pulled away from me, pulled up his clothes and stepped backwards to the entrance hall.

I tidied myself up, rubbing my arse as I turned around to walk back down to where he stood.

"Your leg's fine, isn't it?"

"Yep."

"Cheeky fucker!" He held the door open for me.

As I left the house, I turned to face him. "Good fucker yourself."

So that was Monday.

Now, let me see, what happened Tuesday? Oh! The building site. I know what you're thinking: this sort of thing doesn't happen, not except in porn films. Well, God's honest truth, it happened to me.

There I was, Tuesday morning, sitting in my kitchen and staring out the window, when a group of builders arrived to dig a hole in the road, or fill a hole in, or paint some lines on the road. I don't remember. I don't really care. Anyway, I was sipping my coffee and thinking how it's such a shame that builders in real life are always in their fifties with man boobs and a paunch and about as sexy as a kiss from your granny at Christmas, when what happens?

I'll tell you what happens. Spanish builder in his thirties. That's what happens. Builder's overalls, hi-viz yellow jacket, the nicest arms I've seen in real life for months. He was the youngest in the group by, like, twenty years, and they were all making him do all the difficult jobs, sending him off to get drinks, running and fetching and carrying while the others stood around, resting on their tools.

Another day off sick at home, I couldn't just sit there watching daytime TV and wanking to the internet; not again. So...I decided to have some fun.

I filled a couple of bags with some old clothes, books and DVDs I didn't want anymore—had been meaning to take them to the charity shop for ages—and, one in each hand, I walked very slowly past the builders, making a big show of how hard it was while using my crutches.

An elderly lady tapped my shoulder. "Would you like a hand, son?"

Yes, but not your sort of hand. "I'll be fine, don't worry," I said with a smile and carried on slowly hobbling past the builders. As I reached where they were doing their thing, I stopped, and leant against a lamppost, wiping my brow of the imaginary sweat I'd worked up, and put down the two bags. I caught the attention of Spanish builder man and rolled my eyes.

My guess that he was new and kind was right. While the other builders leant on their spades and smoked cigarettes or flicked through *The Sun* or *The Mirror*, Spanish guy walked over to me. His long, wavy, brown hair peeked out the bottom of his yellow cap.

"Can I carry for you?" he asked in a rich Spanish accent, all deep-brown eyes and thick, dark lips.

"Thank you so much," I replied, doing my best man-damsel-in-distress impression. I pointed round the corner and explained I was trying to get to the Oxfam not far away. If I could get him out of sight of the other builders, I could move on to stage two.

A few moments later, we were round the corner and had been talking about the weather being so much colder than in Spain and how I'd broken my leg. I told him it was a decorating accident, and he offered to decorate my place for me if I needed it.

I puffed and panted and sat on a nearby bench.

He sat next to me.

I pulled my phone from my pocket and opened a dating app, scrolled through a few pages of men and picked the closest man to me at that moment. "Are you Spain underscore eighty-two?"

"Si."

"Do you want to make an invalid man very happy?"

He glanced at his watch and gestured with his head back to his other builder friends.

"They think you're helping me."

We went to one of the builders' tents a few streets away, which he knew would be empty. At first, I was worried about someone walking in, but once Spanish guy unzipped his flies to reveal his curvy cock among a dark nest of wiry hairs, I soon forgot that. He pulled my cock through my flies and knelt in front of me, taking me deep into his throat while squeezing my balls. Then he turned me around and started licking my balls and moving down until he was tonguing my arse. I like a bit of rimming as much as the next man, but I wanted to get back to his big bendy Spanish cock, so I pulled him from his knees and, grabbing his cock with one hand and his balls with the other, I wanked him as hard as I could.

His eyes showed me how much he wanted to keep tonguing my arse, but the wind was blowing into the tent, and I was keen to finish and get back home for a strong coffee and a nap on the sofa. I put his hands on my cock, showed him how I wanted him to wank me, and before long, we were standing opposite each other, wanking in unison, staring into each other's eyes and breathing each other's hot breath. Before long, he came all over my T-shirt and I came all over his navel. He wiped himself with a tissue, straightened his clothes and left the tent without looking back, shaking his head from side to side.

No matter. I assembled myself into as presentable a way as possible given the circumstances, then checked no one was looking and walked the few streets back home. As I passed the building site, I tried to catch Spanish guy's eyes, but he stared resolutely at the ground as he dug the hole with all the concentration of someone trying to understand E equals MC squared or whatever it is.

I jumped into the shower once home and afterwards dozed on the sofa with a mug of coffee by my side. The builders were finished by Thursday.

Wednesday…I had a day off, despite trying to tempt Spanish builder again, messaging him on the app. He blocked me, so I stuck with the internet and remained alone for the day.

Thursday, as the builders finished, I felt that familiar itch of horniness again, picked up my crutches and got on a bus to a pub in Soho.

Within fifteen minutes, I was being bought drinks by a bear in his late forties. A well-preserved late forties. Grey beard, no hair, leather harness and, sad to notice, grey generic brand jeans.

Colin, I think he was called, bought us drinks and we quickly established what we both wanted.

I explained I hadn't been out in a long time, gesturing to my leg and crutches and said I wanted some fun.

"I've just moved out from my ex, so nothing complicated," he said, grabbing his groin and squeezing what I noticed to be a reasonable-sized bulge.

Conveniently, he lived in Covent Garden—a little mews house near the covered market. He showed me to the bathroom, told me to wash.

I met him in the kitchen, a towel wrapped around my waist, propped on crutches, where he stood, a drink in both hands, wearing nothing except grey socks and a cock ring.

He handed me a drink, then removed my towel before stabbing his erection into my stomach.

"What about your harness?" I asked, noticing it was gone, and there wasn't any evidence of any BDSM accoutrements in the flat either.

"I'm not really into it. He was, and I suppose I stick with it 'cos it's part of who I am. But it's not really part of who I am. Isn't it funny when you're not who you thought you were before?"

This was far too deep for what I wanted. I wanted to fuck and go, not to be someone's relationship counsellor. To stop him talking, I pushed him to his knees and pushed my cock into his mouth, thrusting a few times to get myself hard…and screeching a few times as his teeth scraped me.

The rest passed without much note, but let me just say: that afternoon, despite feeling not too in the mood, I managed to make that sad-looking forty-something man very happy. OK, so, I thought of Zac Efron to keep myself hard while I fucked him, and he wanted to cuddle me afterwards *then* started talking about meeting for coffee sometime, but I ploughed on, fucked him good, and left within an hour, throwing his business card down the drain as I crossed Covent Garden.

So that was Thursday. Friday night, I was exhausted, and stayed in, had an early night alone.

And that brings us right up to now: Saturday night. Bjorn is coming round to see how I'm recovering and keep me company. Another quiet one, I'm sure. He's bringing some Swedish meatballs he's made, and I'm providing a Dime bar chocolate tart I bought from Ikea.

My phone is ringing; it's him now.

***

I let Bjorn into the flat, all six and a half feet of him, long blond straight hair swept over one side of his square head, blue eyes, wide smile, a sleeveless white T-shirt one size too small and dark jeans straining at the thighs.

He kissed me, with tongues and squeezed my bum. "No Angie here tonight?"

"Dubai, Mumbai, Shanghai, goodbye. She's been doing lots of extra shifts lately—I've hardly seen her. Wants to get a new car. I've been fending for myself all alone." I smiled at the memory of the week so far.

We ate the food, then flicked through the channels for something to watch.

"We don't have to watch a film," Bjorn said. He stared into my eyes and did that thing he always did during warm-ups before we danced together; he flexed his biceps and pectoral muscles, causing his left then right pec to dance slightly up and down, all the while smiling at me.

"I'm tired. Let's watch a film," I replied, desperately trying to dampen down my increasingly stiffening cock.

"You don't have to do much. You are in recovery. You are here to be looked after. Let me look after you." He removed my T-shirt, and his, and continued with the muscle flexing as he gently pulled me onto my back. Laying me on the sofa with my legs across his lap, he undid my flies and top button and pulled my pants to one side so my cock could breathe easily and peek up towards his mouth.

"I've missed this," he said. "Much better for your rehab than watching a film." And then he was sucking my cock and taking me into his mouth and out again in a flowing rhythm while massaging my balls and pushing oh so gently yet firmly into my prostate. As I threw my head back, I don't remember thinking anything more than how I didn't want that pleasure to end ever.

Did I just lie there like a stunned mullet and let him do all the work? I did at first, but after a while I couldn't resist his magnificent body so I pulled him off me, and with a bit of manoeuvring, we lay top to tail on the sofa, our heads bobbing on each other's cocks as the pleasure built from my groin. With my mouth full of him and my nostrils filled with his distinctive musky smell, it all came flooding back to me.

He put his head back. "You want me to fuck, or you to fuck me?"

That was Bjorn. Always straight to the point. I loved that about him—among other things.

I knew how good he was at both of those options since we'd flip-flopped the last few times he'd come round mine to 'watch a film'; I'd felt his presence in my insides for days afterwards. Fan-fucking-tastic, it was. But now, on this Saturday evening, when

I was meant to be recovering, I shook my head and simply said, "This is good. No?"

To which he replied, "It is good, yes," before licking my balls as he tugged my cock with his hand.

Afterwards, we lay on the sofa in a sweaty, salty, sticky heap, head to tail, stroking each other's legs and stomachs. When it was apparent neither of us were able to go again quite so soon, we moved so we were sitting next to each other, under a blanket I'd told him to fetch from a cupboard.

We watched half a film—I don't remember which it was—before his hands returned to my body. Although my mind wanted to rest, to simply be, my cock had other ideas, and we sat on the sofa, our legs wide open, balls to balls, wanking each other off, the blanket long since thrown on the floor.

I don't want you thinking he forced me into any of that. Oh no. No one forces *me* to have sex. And it wasn't as if that was all he did. We talked about The Accident, of the falling glitter ball on stage, and the St John Ambulance man and his carrying me to the changing room, the banter we'd had and Ambulance Man disappearing.

I'd told Bjorn I'd seen something in Troy's eyes. "I don't know what it was when he carried me to the changing room. He stared at me. And I swear he was smelling me."

"Disgusting. That is weird," Bjorn said, scrunching up his face.

"Weird for a straight man, yes."

"I will be glad when you are back to work. This time you spend alone is not good for you, I think." He stared around the living room at piles of DVDs and pizza boxes.

"He was sexy. Like proper porn-film sexy." My eyes glinted.

"Was he as big as me? Does he go to the gym, do you think?" Bjorn flexed his pectoral muscles to emphasise his point.

"There's no way of knowing, is there? I shan't see him again. Why would I? Still, it makes a good story to tell down the pub, I suppose."

"Another straight man tourist, is this what you say?"

I nodded at the phrase I'd given the men I slept with who, during the throws of passion, while they were in me, or indeed when I was in them, were no-holds-barred, loving the gay sex to bits. But once it was all over, they claimed to be straight. Phrases often thrown about were 'it's just sex' or 'I don't do it often', or my favourite 'what I do in bed isn't what I am in the world' and variations on that theme. It would make my blood boil— these men who wanted to get a bit of cock because it was easier to pull a man than a woman, and then disappear back to their straight lives, taking the piss out of us gays along with the other homophobic twats.

"You are, I think, best to not see him again." Bjorn paused, continuing to flex his muscles at me as he stood in the middle of the room, posed like a model on the front of *Men's Health* magazine.

"You're right. End of speculation." But I had definitely felt something from Troy, a connection I hadn't felt from the 'straight' men I'd slept with. A connection deeper and more emotional than what I'd had with a lot of gay guys I'd been with, actually, as sad as that sounds. It had been an easy, natural comfort we'd created together in a short time, in that room, after that accident. Now I thought about it, it seemed sad to never be able to revisit that again, even if it would only have been for friendship. I could be friends with a straight man. I was so certain of it that I told Bjorn so.

"Why bother if you do not fuck with him?" he said. And then, with a waggle of his eyebrows in time with his waggling pecs, and with all the inevitability of night following day or a fumble in the bushes at a gay pride festival, we were naked again, all thoughts of Troy long since gone from our minds.

CHAPTER 8

Troy

IN THE KITCHEN, Olive was introducing me to a new kitchen assistant who'd just started. As Olive described the jobs the new girl would be doing, all I noticed was how she looked like a younger, prettier version of Freya—bobbed blonde hair to her shoulders, light, freckly face and slim build with smallish breasts underneath the black apron Olive had given her. *I wonder if they are a B cup? I wonder if her breasts are like Freya's in size? I wonder...*

"Troy!" Olive shouted to get my attention. "I was saying Carley here's new to the area. Could do with someone to show her around. I thought, since you've been here a while and live local, you might like to do that." She raised her eyebrows at me, then winked.

I stared at the ground, wishing it would open up and swallow me. What made her think Carley was what I needed to get over Freya?

"I'm pretty busy at the moment. The gardens used to be looked after by three full-time staff, but now it's only me. And I've got to get a lot ready for the public open days—make sure the picnic areas are mowed and the flowerbeds by the car park are perfect. I'm under strict instructions from Her Upstairs."

Carley smiled at me quickly then put her hands in the pockets of her apron.

Olive goaded, "Come on, it won't take long. Just where to find somewhere to rent—she's in the staff bedrooms at the moment. Where to get a decent meal…"

"I don't want a younger sports car," I muttered to myself as I strode to the door. "I don't want a sports car at all." I left the building and mowed the lawns at top speed on the sit-on mower, cutting the heads off the flowers near the grass and nearly tipping the mower over on a few corners.

***

A few days later, I found myself, one lunchtime, walking into the nearby village and explaining to Carley the intricacies of the post office and that any parcels she took delivery of there would be news in the village that day.

"Thanks," she said. "I know you're busy. I told Olive to leave it, said I'd be fine, but this is helpful. Thing is, you don't know what you don't know when you're new to a place, do you?"

Not knowing what to say, I simply explained that if she wanted to get a good pick of places to rent, she'd need to make friends with the estate agent in the next town or by the time she saw anything online it would all be gone. I handed her a piece of paper with the estate agent's details.

She held it and my hand in both of hers and stared up at me with light-blue eyes and a small smile. "It's nice to have a friend here." She pulled my face close to hers and kissed me, her soft lips pressed against mine, her smooth skin next to my stubbly chin and her sweet perfume smell filling my nostrils. "Can I take you for lunch as a thank you?" she asked eventually, after pulling back from the kiss.

"Yeah. I'd like that." And, because it was the right thing to do—the thing I should have done before, since splitting up with Freya—I returned the kiss, really putting my back into it. I breathed in her smell and reached behind her to grab her bum. I closed my eyes and let myself be in the moment.

It was some scene from that rom com Freya had made me watch with Hugh Grant and Julia Roberts, only, unlike in that film, I felt nothing. In fact, worse than nothing, I felt repulsion for Carley—beautiful, pretty Carley. Where I'd expected to feel the excitement and butterflies in my stomach, it felt as sexy as imagining the prime minister in the nude on the toilet.

All of these thoughts flashed through my brain in an instant, and I pulled back from the kiss, held my hands up and said, "Sorry. My fault. Wrong of me. I'm forty. I'm just out of a long relationship. Don't know what I want. You're best off avoiding me—I would if I was you. Steer well clear." I ran away, leaving her outside the village shop where, just a few moments ago, everything had seemed so certain, so clear, so normal.

***

Dear Dave,

It's been a while since I wrote. There's not been much to say of late, I suppose—working, sleeping, settled into my new place now. Little room of my own. No girly things there either. All my own stuff, as I want it, where I want it. Not that there's much of it. Made a great big fucking tit of myself with this new bird at work, Carley. Should've kept well clear, but stupidly thought I'd get in there and get over Freya by getting stuck into Carley.

Was I shy? No, I'm not shy. I kissed her and I felt my dick shrivelling, pulling back into my body. What's going on with me? Women have fucked up my head so much I'm keeping my distance from all of 'em I suppose.

Been worried about this Julian bloke, his bang on the head—is he back at work? Is he dancing again? Did a bit of research, looked him up and found he has his own website—not Facebook, but his own proper website julianbarnes-dancer.com. It's well impressive—lists who he's danced for, how long he's been dancing, what sorts of dance training he's had. More than he told me, actually. Interesting to read it all.

Anyway, I thought I'd drop him a note, see how he is, if he's back on his feet, if he's back dancing, if he's got any dizziness. I told him at the time about that, and blurry vision—those are the things to worry about with head injuries, only he'd just had a head injury so he might not have remembered that. Joked that it was all part of the service—aftercare, I said! Lol. I ended it with a smiley face. Friendly. Not too much. I know he kissed me, but you don't put kisses to another bloke in an email, do you? NO fucking way. Wonder if he's replied yet.

Checked emails and nothing. I'll leave it. Might just friend him on Facebook—put a note of who I am, he won't remember me, I'm sure. I hardly remember him, really. Not much.

Fuck's sake, I've written all that about nothing. Anyway, night now, early start at work—fixing the fuck-ups I made earlier this week. Trying to garden when angry comes back to bite you in the bum. And this weekend I'm volunteering, so busy. Might be a while till I'm back.

CHAPTER 9

Julian

BERLIN—PART OF SALLIE's Europe tour. I'd said it might be a bit much for me, first job back from being off, but the tour manager said I should get on with it and stop making such a mountain out of a molehill.

I was about to point out it was my molehill to make, and that I'd been very ill, but remembered how much I needed the money and instead kept quiet.

Fair enough, four weeks off work was milking it a bit.

After the show, I ran off stage...well, walked quickly, being a bit careful of my leg, and declined Bjorn and the other boys' offer of a trip to a gay club,

"Come on, they've got a hard house dance floor and dark rooms if you fancy."

"I'm gonna get an early night ready for tomorrow," I said.

"We're here tomorrow. Two more nights in Berlin and then it's off to Paris. Come on, kick back, enjoy yourself."

I shook my head, kissed all the boys on their cheeks, mopped my brow dramatically, complaining of the beginnings of a headache...

Now, I was under the shower in my hotel room.

I dried myself and was relieved at the ache in my muscles after so long with so little to do with my body except wanking and fucking. Surprisingly for me, my first week of *sex, sex, sex* hadn't continued. Not due to the effectiveness of the crutches routine wearing off—oh no, that was still as effective as ever—

but I stopped trying. It was all so exhausting, pretending to be on crutches and then running off to search for another bit of sex, like an animal foraging for food in the forest. Don't get me wrong; I didn't live like a monk for the next three weeks. I got some action, just not the heroic levels of that first week.

Although the promise of a gay club in Berlin was appealing— Bjorn had promised 'plenty of filthy German fuckers wall to wall', based on his past experience—I wasn't in the mood. Not since the first night we'd arrived in Europe and I'd agreed to go out in Spain. I'd woken up in a car outside a night club—the music was still blaring—in the early hours with some guy sucking me off. The feeling was quickly overtaken by sickness, and I pushed him off, opened the door and threw up over the ground only to then somehow make my sorry, lonely way back to the hotel alone. In reception, I was greeted by Sallie and the company manager, the stage manager and some of the techies—lighting and sound guys mainly—who tended to be straight and less interested in going to the gay clubs than the mainly gay dancers.

Sallie turned from who she was talking to at the bar and said, "Walk of shame is it, Julian darling?" She sniffed. "And is that Ralph? Have you Ralphed? Can't keep your drink down?" She sighed. "And there was me, thinking you were one of the old campaigners, one of the more experienced ones, used to life on the road. Looks like with all that time off you've fallen out of practice."

I smiled weakly, feeling the pull of my hotel bed and tasting sick in my mouth. "Night," was all I managed before walking slowly to the lifts and mercifully not meeting anyone else until the following morning.

That was why now, I was sitting on my bed in the silk pyjamas Angie had brought me back from the Middle East on her last long-haul flight, sipping sparkling mineral water and feeling very virtuous indeed.

I clicked on the icon and was soon Skyping Angie, her smiling face and waving hands joining me in my room from thousands of miles away. "Not going out tonight?"

I shook my head and told her about the blow job car incident.

She laughed. "Promise me you'll never change. I don't think I'd be able to cope if you did. It would shake my whole world view, like when they started saying fat was good for you and we shouldn't eat carbs. I threw away all my old diet books. It was like the dawning of a new Jerusalem. Or when they said the nineties were back in fashion. I can't take another of those life-changing shifts. Promise me you won't change."

"Promise. If it makes you feel any better, I've been having flashbacks of going to a gay sauna, a dark room, a club and a bar with Bjorn and the boys, so that's still very much the same."

"Thought you'd had enough of sex when you were off sick."

"I didn't mean to. It was in Spain. They're renowned for being very friendly, and cruisy." Shrugging, I said, "What else was there to do?"

"What you doing tonight?"

I explained how I'd resisted Bjorn and the boys' lures. "Face pack, some channel surfing, then bed."

"Far be it for me to keep you from your evening. I'm away for a bit, but message me if you want to chat again. Feels like I've not seen you physically—person to person, touching hands together—in years."

"Now who's dramatic?" I rolled my eyes.

"Must be rubbing off." She waved and ended the call.

***

On the final leg of the Europe tour, I was sitting on the tour bus, nursing a sore head and an even more sore arse from a long night of partying far too hard, when Bjorn appeared at my side, tiny shorts and a blue vest top out of which he bulged and stretched.

"Sallie demanded I ask you if you're all right," he said, apropos of nothing as far as I was aware.

"What's that meant to mean? Who's she think she is, my mother?" I added the extra formality to the end, instead of the usual 'mum', just for added indignation I couldn't cope with in my delicate state.

"She's worried you'll go too far and you'll fuck it all up. She said she can't afford to have dancers standing at the back like they're there in body but not in spirit."

"She said that?" I pursed my lips. What. A. Bitch.

"Not just to you, to all of us. The tour manager is clamping down. There's been some shit on the internet from fans towards the end of the tour—said they saw a couple of us yawning on stage and one of us fell over, nearly dropped Sallie when we were carrying her into the clam shell at the start of act two."

"How fucking dare they? That wasn't me!" I grabbed Bjorn's hands, terrified for a moment. "Was it?"

"No, and I don't think it was me, but we've both been well below par a few times and it has been noticed."

"She's a fine one to talk, out until the early hours with the promoters, staying up all night on not just coffee and fresh air, if you know what I mean."

Bjorn shot me a look. "You have no evidence of that. You cannot start these rumours."

"Well, the rudeness of it all." I was bristling at the impertinence. "We are consummate professionals, all of us dancers."

"If you can class rolling in at six o'clock the following evening on no sleep, then falling asleep in a warm-up dance class and forgetting the first two costume changes—'a consummate professional' was it you said?—then we are."

"I did not," I spat, turning away from this assault on my senses, my life…my everything, really.

I SHOULD BE SO LUCKY

"No, but two of the others did, and we've both done nearly as bad. It is a warning for us to be a bit more careful. I think this is all it is."

"Good job I stayed in a bit more lately, then."

"I was wondering about that. Why? Did you not want to sample some hot Swedish cock? And you missed out on Spain, didn't you?"

"The blow job in the car was in Spain." I sighed deeply and leant backwards on the seat that irritatingly didn't adjust any further back so I could sleep. "I think I'm going to take a bit of a break from all this cruising. It's a bit like being on a merry-go-round."

"This I have to see. We must try this next time I come to yours." Bjorn waggled his eyebrows and winked.

"Honestly, it's not dirty. It wasn't a double entendre. I meant it's constantly going round. One night, a new place, a new bar, a new man, a new shag. The next night, a new bar, another new man, another new shag. It carries on going round and round. I want to get off the ride for a bit."

Bjorn felt my forehead. "Are you all right? Do you have a sickness? Shall I call the doctor? Julian, *I fucked my way around Europe, twice*, is hanging up his shagging shoes? Are you going soft, getting old?"

"Fuck off! I'm not old. I'm barely thirty."

"Thirty-six."

"But I can pass for a well-preserved thirty. I think it's time for a change." I folded my arms. "I'm done with men."

"Completely? No more men at all?"

"Specifically, I mean, the merry-go-round of endless new men."

"Have you gone and fallen for someone?"

I didn't reply.

"Julian, Mister *I don't do boyfriends, why would anyone want a boyfriend, why would anyone want to fuck the same person for the rest of their life when there's a whole world of men to fuck out there, waiting for me to fuck…"*

I flinched slightly at my most often quoted phrase and justification for my whole being for the past…well, for the whole time since I'd come out, since I was eighteen. Making it eighteen years of men. Swallowing, I considered that for a moment.

"Who is it?" Bjorn asked.

I had been trying to work out how to tell him who was on my mind and not quite managing to assemble the words in a way that wouldn't result in him slapping me around the face and telling me to listen to myself.

"Tell me. I need to know who's bringing an end to our little film nights. I *assume* there will be no more film nights if you are seeing someone." Bjorn stared at me.

"Haven't got that far yet. Early days. It's not really at boyfriend stage. Don't think it ever will be." I stared back at him and smiled the cheekiest smile I could drag up.

"You are joking? The fireman? Still you are thinking about him? He saved you, he talked to you, that's it. You will not hear from him again. And here you are, moping around, missing out on some of the best Swedish cock you could have, all because of some man you spoke to months ago."

"I can't stop thinking about him. There was…something between us. A connection. I can't explain it. The way he stared at me. The way we talked. I've never had that before, not with anyone."

"Oh, thanks. And here is me, thinking we are friends."

"We are. And friends with benefits—good benefits, don't get me wrong. But this was different."

"I can tell you how it was different—he was straight. And you are like a moth to a flame with straight men. Cannot resist trying to convert them, collecting them like moths in a jar."

"I know this. I've been here before. I've been the sex toy of a straight man who's actually gay and homophobic. And I swore

I'd never do it again. Left me feeling like absolute shit, used and dirty, and not in a good way, let me tell you."

"So why do you do this?"

"Because there was something there. I know I shouldn't, because he's either straight and I'll fall in love with a straight man and that's always messy, or he's a straight-acting gay guy who's as homophobic as those knuckle-dragging skinheads I always seem to attract when I'm in straight bars." After a few moments' thinking, I added, "Bi? I'd not considered that before."

Bjorn folded his arms and turned away. "This, is pointless. I do not spend any more time on this. You will not see him again. So that, I say, is good, and it is an end to it. Back to me and you and our film nights together. They were not so bad, were they?"

I thought about the various times Bjorn and I had enjoyed 'film nights' at mine. It was undeniable they were fun. They must have been fun or I wouldn't have done it again and again with him. And, fair enough, he was in the top ten percent in terms of good looks when it came to men I'd slept with—definitely in the top five percent in terms of technique—so what was stopping me just going out with him?

As I turned this thought around in my mind, wondering why it hadn't occurred to me before, and whether I'd actually been missing the most obvious thing all this time, that my friend Bjorn was actually who I was meant to be with—if indeed I was meant to be with anyone—I absentmindedly scrolled through my phone, checking Facebook and messages and then my emails. I noticed a message from someone who'd contacted my website.

Bjorn said, "We could give it a go. Me and you. People always say we are like best friends. Are we not? And we fit together in bed, do we not? So, what is there to lose?" He shrugged.

And then it occurred to me why me and Bjorn didn't make sense. It was all over his face. He didn't really want to be with me, not as boyfriends. He was only doing it because he was afraid of losing me as a friend, as a 'film night' friend, and if I was going to go to all the effort of abandoning my whole belief system and betraying eighteen years of fucking my way around the world—Europe mainly, actually—then I wanted it to be for someone who wanted to be with me as much as I wanted to be with them. Sadly, despite his pectoral twitching, amazing lip action and ability to fuck for hours on end without a pause, Bjorn didn't fit into that category.

"He's just emailed me."

"Who is this?" Bjorn frowned.

"St John Ambulance man—Troy."

"Why?"

"Some shit about aftercare."

"Really?" Shaking his head, Bjorn said, "This, I do not believe."

"That's what he says. But me and you both know that's a big old load of bollocks."

CHAPTER 10

Julian

AND THAT WAS how, a few days later, I found myself meeting Troy under the clock at Liverpool Street station in London, standing on the white floor as thousands of commuters did the fast walk as if they were running that everyone in London seemed to always do.

I checked my watch. Ten minutes late. Bjorn was right, I would never see Troy again. All a waste of time. What a waste of a new outfit. I looked down at my clothes, each item carefully chosen to show him I had made an effort, but not a date-ish effort. Not a possible-boyfriend effort. Oh no. This was a matey, friendly, *wanting to make an effort for someone because he was a friend* sort of effort. Brown chinos and a plain blue T-shirt with a black leather jacket I'd picked up in a vintage shop in Camden. I thought it made me look quite bikery—a touch of the James Dean. This, I had reasoned, would appeal to Troy, from a purely man's man, manly interest point of view, you understand.

But all that was wasted now. I might as well have stayed in the grey sweatpants and frayed white T-shirt I wore when lounging around on the sofa—even when Bjorn came round for one of our 'film' nights.

I turned to walk back to the Tube station and make my way home, bumping into someone—a stupid man who wasn't looking where he was going, too focused on the bunch of flowers he was carrying along with a box of some description. Stupid man.

"All right?" the stupid man asked, resting his hand on my arm.

My eyes trailed along his arm up to his face, where I met the smile. Not quite the smile that launched a thousand ships or any of that shit, but certainly one that made my heart beat a bit faster. And the eyes—deep blue, with crinkles at the outer edges carrying up from his wide, white-teethed smile.

"These are for you." He handed me the flowers—carnations, pink and white—and the box of chocolates. "I wasn't sure what to get. I mean, I know we said it wasn't anything funny. Not ha-ha funny, but you know what I mean." He carried on talking twenty to the dozen about how he'd worried it would be too much for two men to meet in public with flowers and chocolate, and if he should have come as he was, alone, with maybe a paperback so we'd recognise each other, then he realised we'd seen each other before, so that wasn't needed. "'Snot like it's a blind." He coughed, avoiding the next word. "'Cos we've seen each other, haven't we?"

After his initial first email about aftercare and wanting to see if I was OK after the accident, I'd replied and asked if he did this for all his patients. He said he didn't and admitted he just wanted to see me again. On the phone, he'd tried to explain wanting to meet up to see me—"I dunno what it is. Like the first time we met. Laugh, go on, laugh at me. Go for a drink. Have a chat. Mates. Stupid Troy...I don't know what I'm on about, do I?"

Of course I hadn't laughed. In fact, I'd been pretty flattered at this awkward galumphing straight man saying he thought we had a connection. OK, so he hadn't said exactly those words, because, he was...well, he was an awkward galumphing straight man. But between the lines of his emails, that's what I knew he meant.

Now, he shook my hand, firm, tight grip. My mind immediately went south, and I told myself off for having such a sewer-like imagination.

He was still talking about the fucking chocolates and the fucking flowers and saying something about how he didn't ask anyone what to do, because he couldn't. "I don't know what I'd have told anyone. Don't know what it is. So I couldn't do the usual—ask a mate what to do. So this is why I fucked it up." He pointed to the flowers and chocolates. "Look, I'll take 'em back. Give 'em here. I'll put 'em in the bin." He tried to take them off me.

"Leave it out, will you? No one died. For fuck's sake, if you're this tied up in knots over flowers and chocolate, we might as well give up now." I stared at him, taking in his bulky six-foot-six frame, wide shoulders and little bits of chest hair sprouting over the collar of his un-ironed—I noticed—shirt. He had a few stray long eyebrows and could have done with a bit of plucking action around the nose area. Definitely straight. Bless. "Chill out, all right? I am not going to jump on you. Promise. Not all gay men are man-eaters." I laughed to myself.

He laughed quietly, avoiding eye contact and stuffing his hands deep into his pockets.

The tightness of his thighs in his trousers and the bulging of his groin made me lose my train of thought for a few moments. Now, where was I...

"Man-eaters," he said, with a smile.

"See this." I pointed to a scar below my left eye.

He nodded. Another smile. Another flash of the teeth, another crinkling of the edges of his blue eyes.

Another fluttering of my heart. *For fuck's sake, Julian what are you like?* I wished I'd had a wank before coming out—always used to do wonders to dissipate sexual tension, make me think a bit more with the head on my shoulders rather than my other, smaller head. Only this time, because it wasn't anything—well, not quite 'not' anything, as I was finding out, but it wasn't a date—that would have required me emptying my tanks, I hadn't.

"What about it?" He pointed to my scar.

"Ah, yes. My little souvenir from coming on to a straight man who seemed a bit bendy. Never again."

"I'm not a bit bendy. If that's what you think, it's better I go." He stared at me, then the floor.

I shrugged, because, on Bjorn's advice, once he'd agreed to me going through with meeting Troy, his one caveat had been to take it all on first appearances. Whatever Troy says, I should believe

55

and not try to bend the truth or try to read something into it that wasn't there.

Now, Troy suggested we go to a pub. "Fancy a pint?" His eyebrows raised optimistically.

"A drink, yes, but not a pint. You lead the way."

He strode off in front of me, occasionally glancing at his phone to check he was going in the right direction.

I noted from the rear he gave me a pleasing view; his wide shoulders tapered to a narrow waist and a pair of well-rounded arse cheeks tightly encased in jeans that led to two slightly bow-legged thighs and feet that stuck out at ninety degrees to each other. His arms, when not holding the phone out for directions, were held a few inches from his body, swinging back and forth as he walked.

Naturally I popped an instant hard-on and had to take off my jacket so I could hold it in front of my groin to disguise it.

Face value. Repeat after me, Julian, face value.

In my experience, straight men were rarely aware of how sexy they were, simply just by being straight. And this, I always found, was half the attractiveness. Once they became aware of how insane they were driving you with their animal magnetism and posturing masculinity, they usually transformed into a preening, smug cocky idiot, and that—despite how physically sexy they were—was always very unattractive. Mercifully, Troy appeared completely oblivious to this.

I pulled my jacket closer to myself and sped up so I was walking next to him, therefore not seeing the spectacular rear view that had caused me to get in the awkward situation in the first place.

***

Once in the pub—full of suited city gentlemen shouting at one another or into their mobile phones—Troy went to the bar to buy the first round of drinks. "It's a cask-ale-on-tap pub. Don't think they'll do a cosmopolitan, or a Long Island Iced Tea," he'd said as we arrived.

I shrugged and told him to get me whatever he was getting. After his awkwardness at the flowers, I thought it was my turn to feel a bit like a fish out of Soho.

He put two foaming pints of beer onto the dark wooden table and sat opposite me, his legs wide open as he perched on the stool. "Get that down you." He took a long sip, and his Adam's apple bobbed up and down his freshly shaved neck.

In for a penny, in for a pound, I copied him. The first sip hit my taste buds, reminding me why people called beer 'bitter'. I swallowed and took another sip, getting used to its taste; by the end of the fourth, I was starting to quite enjoy it.

"Been here before?" Troy asked after I'd been staring at the beer mats on the walls for several minutes.

"No."

"Sorry. Should've asked where you wanted to go. I just assumed…"

I put my hand on his as it rested on the table, then quickly removed it. "It's enough making you schlep on a train to London without dragging you to some bar in Soho or Vauxhall. It's all right. Not much different from how I remember it."

"It was easier here than getting on the Tube. Train from Essex only took forty-five minutes. I'll get a cab back from the station." He looked at his pint.

"What do you do in Essex? The St John Ambulance is voluntary, isn't it? What do you do for money?"

He told me about being a gardener for a country estate in Essex—not one I'd heard of, but then again, why would I? Essex, being outside the M25, may as well have been Scotland for all the likelihood of me going there. Full of Darrens and Sharons and covered in concrete. What the hell would I want with Essex?

"Enjoy it?" I asked, because, to be honest, once he'd mentioned gardening and country estates, I knew I was a bit lost. These were not familiar topics of conversation. I didn't talk to any of my gay friends about shit like this, and the guys I'd picked up—well, conversation was rarely the first thing on our minds.

Troy talked about the household, and how he'd worked there for seven years, and about the cook, Olive, who was like a house mother to him and the other younger staff. He said the family who owned the house basically left him to it; he didn't need to talk to them much. They didn't care as long as he mowed the lawns, planted the flowers and other gardening-related things he mentioned which, without any reference points, just slipped from my mind.

By now, I'd been up to buy a round twice, and Troy had been up at least once more, so we must have been on our third or fourth pint each.

I checked my watch: still early enough to get to Soho and see who was about, or pick up someone; enough time to save what was left of the evening. As cute as Troy was, so far, the conversation had hardly been riveting, and if all I wanted was sexy men's behinds to look at, I could easily get that from the internet without spending nearly an hour listening to gardening stories.

Just as I was about to make my excuses to leave—claiming I'd had a text from a friend in his hour of need which was actually from Bjorn asking how it was going and if I fancied a quick bunk-up back at his place—Troy said, "You don't wanna hear about me. What about you? What's it like being a dancer for Sallie? Is she really like she seems on the TV?" He paused.

I shifted on my chair, wondering if another twenty minutes would matter to Bjorn and hoping Troy didn't ask me to get Sallie's autograph. *If he asks that I'll leave straight away.* That, as far as I was concerned, was the height of naff and had been the cause of many an 'oh, sorry, I've got to go' moment before.

He leant forward, put his arms on the table, and grabbed my hands. "I ain't never met a bloke like you before. Not properly—to talk to, like. It's a whole new world. Dancing for money. Working with celebrities."

I stared down at his large, hairy hands and crossed my legs to dampen my ardour. "She doesn't like celebrity. Says it's naff.

She's a singer, dancer, pop princess. She prefers it 'cos it's more specific."

He saluted. "Got it. Pop princess. What's it like, then?" He returned his hand to its previous position on top of mine and stroked my skin. *Stick to surface small-talk conversations* was what Bjorn had advised too. I told him about Sallie's bollocking of a group of us for partying too hard, and how she worried about us, like her own younger brothers or something.

"What had you lot been up to, partying around Europe?" His eyes widened. He was still holding my hands.

My heart beat faster. My palms were sweating; I worried he'd notice and remove his hands from mine. He didn't. I told him some of the stories from the European tour, some involving me, some involving Bjorn and the other guys. *We're just friends, why keep any of my more shameful sexual exploits from a mate?* That was what I told myself. At peak confusion about the hand-holding and attentiveness, I deliberately dropped a bomb into the conversation to see how he'd react. "He's my fuck buddy."

"Who is?" Troy asked.

"Bjorn. If we can't be arsed to go out and pull when we're on tour or don't find anyone, we take care of each other's needs. It's just sex, so it's simple." I shrugged casually.

He stared at me for a few moments. "And you're friends too? You said earlier he'd texted you, and you might meet him later."

Had I? I probably had. He really had been listening. "Haven't you ever stayed friends with an ex? Or slept with a friend?"

He shook his head. "Haven't seen Freya since I left. And the ex before that? Nope. And before her? No. Why would I?"

"If I stopped being friends with all the men I'd slept with, I couldn't be friends with most of London. And where would that leave me?"

"I know sex and love are separate. It's just I've never managed to convince any girlfriends." He paused, leant back, separated our hands and then clasped and unclasped his hands together a few times, pausing to look at the nails. "That's why I wanted to keep it…" He looked at me. "Simple."

I see, that's what I am, is it? Simple. Well, I was happy with a bit of simple, especially encased in a body like his. "That's how my and Bjorn's arrangement works. If I call for him to come round and he wants to, he knows what it's for. If he doesn't want it, no problem. He's not my fucking boyfriend. And that means we can be totally honest with each other. Take tonight—" I stopped myself, biting my tongue, realising I was letting my mouth run away with the beer.

Troy shifted around the table, so he was sitting next to me. I felt the warmth of his body. I smelt the mixture of his eau de toilette—he'd have called it cologne, I was sure—and his own distinctive man-musky smell. I was close enough to see where he'd missed a few bits shaving his neck and face. There was a small cut to the right of his Adam's apple, and I reached out to touch it.

He held my hand as it touched his neck. "What did Bjorn have to say about tonight?"

"Not much." I stared into his eyes.

We sat like that for a few moments until, finally, Troy said, "I can't stop thinking about you. I don't know what it is."

"But you're straight."

"There is this girl—woman—at work. Carley. Olive thought I'd get on well with her. She's nice. Similar looking to Freya, but I stopped myself."

"Why? Best way to get over someone is to get under—or on top of—someone else. It's an oldie, but it's a goodie."

"Didn't seem fair."

"On who?"

Troy shrugged and gestured to the bar.

I shrugged back, realising I was pretty drunk already and not wanting to stop the momentum of this part of the conversation.

"One more. I'll get us one more each." He stood, knocking the chair back so it fell on the floor. While he bought the drinks, I righted the chair and texted Bjorn to tell him there had been a change of plan and things were getting interesting this end.

He immediately texted back: *face value—remember this.*

Troy sat next to me, pressing himself against my side as he slid my drink in front of me. He took a long sip of his pint, swallowing down a quarter of it in one go. I stared at the nick on his neck where I'd touched a while ago and realised I didn't have a clue what I was doing. I didn't know what any of Troy's revelation about not being able to stop thinking about me actually meant, and I suddenly felt very lost in the whole situation. Horny straight man, I could handle—fuck and go. Teasing straight man, I could handle too—tell him to fuck off and go get myself a gay playmate for the evening. Emotional straight man? This was a combination I'd not encountered before, unless you counted the ones where it had all been a precursor to the 'my girlfriend doesn't understand me' speech, which really was a variation on the horny straight man version.

I didn't want to scare Troy off, but at the same time, I felt a sudden sense of danger and excitement. Me being me, I relished the danger and edged a few inches closer to Troy on the bench so our legs were touching.

"It's what everyone expects of you when you look like me. I was six foot and hairy by the time I was sixteen. First one in my class at secondary school to shave. People used to point and say stuff in the communal showers. Everyone else had smooth, boyish bodies, and there was me, sixteen, covered in hair and fully grown. Everywhere."

The image emblazoned on my mind but I quickly dismissed it, returning to the issue in hand. I bit my lip and nodded for him to continue. I didn't want to say too much in case I scared him off, like a baby deer. I had become the straight-man whisperer or something. When I told Bjorn my technique, he'd be trying it out in the gym changing room as soon as I could say bulging Lycra.

"I went camping. Me and my best mate. We did everything together. He didn't take the piss out of me at school. He wasn't as developed as me then, but by eighteen, he'd caught up—mostly. Anyway, we went camping in the forest, and we were talking about girls we fancied at school. The ones with the biggest tits, that sort of thing. He was going out with one and was telling me how they'd kissed at her place all night while her parents were out, lying on the sofa, and he had a stiffy for the whole night. All he wanted her to do was finish him off. Not go the full way. His balls were aching, he said.

"You know how it is—talking about sex gets you revved up, doesn't it? The fire was crackling between us as we lay on our sleeping bags on the ground. He said how he'd gone home that night and, because he couldn't sleep, he'd lay in his bed and in a few seconds had finished himself off. A few quick tugs was all it took.

"He asked if I'd had the same problem. I said I hadn't, because the girls didn't trust me, thought I was only after one thing at school. So, even though I looked like a man, I hadn't done anything with any girls at that point. But there, lying on the sleeping bag, I was bursting. Straining to get out of my pants, I was. And I could see my mate was too, the way he held himself. I don't remember the exact words we said, but we were talking about a few quick tugs and that it didn't mean anything, and we didn't need to tell anyone about it. It was nothing, really. And so, we pushed our trousers and pants down, and we did it." He stopped talking, looked over his shoulder as if someone was going to run in and sweep him away.

"You fucked?"

"No."

"You sucked each other off?" I asked slowly, again mindful of the scaring the baby deer issue.

"No. Just a few tugs was all it took."

"Right."

"He looked at the fire while he did me. Didn't look at me. My face, or my... But I... I wanted to look at his face, the way his eyes closed while I did it, how he was enjoying it. It made me enjoy it more. I wanted to see him. You know. Him."

"His cock?" I said quietly. "You can say it here. I've said much worse in my European stories."

"Yes. His cock. I wanted to." He opened his mouth. "But we talked about that. That was definitely gay, we'd said. But a few tugs, that wasn't."

"I should have a T-shirt with that across the front. How many times have I heard a straight man say that to me?"

He laughed nervously.

"And then what happened?"

"We climbed back into our sleeping bags and went to sleep. In our own tents."

"Of course. Did you stay friends with him afterwards?"

"Oh yeah. We used to joke about it. I jokingly asked if he wanted to do it again, made up some shit about a girlfriend giving me blue balls. But he said he didn't want to make a habit of it."

"And then what?"

"I pushed it to the back of my mind, shagged loads of girls, had loads of girlfriends, lived with girlfriends, went out with them, split up with them. It's always the same—they say I don't want to commit. I'm holding back. I'm waiting for something."

"What are you waiting for? What have you been waiting for?" I hoped he didn't say me, because that would have been far too cheesy to handle and also too much of a big pressure all on me.

"I didn't talk to gay guys—not very many in my lines of work. Don't go to the pubs and that in London. Because, then it would mean I was. But I couldn't be. Look at me." He gestured to himself.

"What do you mean, you couldn't be?"

"I like sport. I hate cooking. I can't stand interior decorating— always brings me out in hives going to Ikea every time I've had to set up home again with another girlfriend. Can't dance. Can't sing. Never been to the theatre—never seen any of those films I'm supposed to like. With the singing. And the dancing. People leaping about and everywhere bursting into song in the middle of everything."

"Musicals?"

"Hate 'em. Always have. I tried, see. And shopping. Clothes. All that. I hate it all. I can't remember the last time I went shopping. Do it all online now. I buy clothes when mine wear out. So I knew I couldn't be, you know?" He blinked slowly and a tear rolled down his cheek. "How can I be?"

"You can be whatever you want to be. Stop worrying about what other people think about you. You're stuck between thinking the gays won't let you into this secret club, and the straights throwing you out of the secret club. Let me tell you a secret." I motioned for him to lean closer and whispered into his ear, inhaling his musky, minty cologne at the same time, "There is no secret. Be who the fuck you want to be."

"What do you mean?" He furrowed his brow.

"My friend Bjorn, if you met him, you'd never think he was a poof. He's well into his gym, goes twice a day, will fight anyone who dares laugh at him, hates musicals, can't cook to save his life, but he's as gay as they come. Some of his tales of heroic pulling while we've been on tour would make your eyes water. Dark rooms, orgies, men as old as his dad, some just eighteen, when he's in the mood, anyone's hole will do as long as it's male. Bjorn is a filthy gay fucker and make no mistake. If you saw him, he's as butch as they come. Not so butch he ends up being camp—I've fucked Muscle Marys with helium heels, trust me. No, he's proper fight-you-in-an-alley, burping-and-farting butch. Mind you, he's a good listener too, so maybe that's where it all comes through on him."

"Oh."

"It's not like there's someone waiting with a clipboard to check off if you meet the criteria to be let into the gays' kingdom. Anything goes."

He put his head in his hands. "I'm such a twat. I can't believe it. All this time I've wasted."

"How were you supposed to know?"

"It wasn't until I talked to you, until I clicked with you. I've never clicked with a man, not like that, not before. Not since my mate, and it was one-way. I've never had another gay guy to try clicking with before."

Oh, shit. I was in so much trouble. All this, all this coming out, I had all this on my narrow gay shoulders. I glanced at Troy's wide shoulders. How come he'd picked me to spill his gay guts to after keeping it to himself for so long? Me? Why?

"Is it really that simple?" He sat back in the chair, straightening his back.

"Is what that simple?"

"Being…you know."

"You can say it. It's not a rude word. How old are you?" I knew this, because he'd told me the first time we'd met, and I'd mentally licked my lips at a more experienced older man.

"Forty. Too old to start again."

"With this Carley bird?"

"And Freya before her, and Sara before her, and Claire before her. A whole list of failed relationships. I can't do it again."

"Now you know why they all failed. No matter how kind and sweet and pretty they were, even if you really put your back into it, there was only so long it would last before something inside you told you it was pointless."

"Because they weren't men."

"Exactly."

"And now I've found you, I can have the relationship I've always wanted." He kissed me, a gentle kiss, his lips pressed against mine, his tongue licking my lips then moving farther into my mouth.

It was what I'd been fantasising about him doing since the first time we'd met. It was exactly how I'd hoped the evening would go. It was perfect. Only there was a nagging doubt in my stomach alongside the large manly hand resting on the inside of my thigh. I pulled away from the kiss.

"It's flattering that I've brought all this out in you. Me, someone who's as deep as a puddle, making you come out. No one at work will believe me. Bjorn will cream his pants. But I don't do boyfriends. Never have, never will."

"Neither have I. Let's find it out together." His face was so optimistic, hopeful, it felt like I was about to kick a puppy downstairs when I next spoke.

"Very funny," I said. "You *have* been in relationships—hundreds of them by the sound of it."

"Tens more like. I've not been with as many people as you have." He winked, with a smile.

"Suppose I walked into that one, didn't I? I've never been in a relationship."

"What about your mate, Bjorn?"

"Friends with benefits. He is not my boyfriend, and I'm not his. If I don't want to see him, I tell him. If I want us to fuck and go, we do just that. If I want to go out with him and have a laugh, I do, and that's where it ends."

"You asked his advice about tonight."

I had. This was an undeniable truth, and one I'd also told Troy not more than an hour ago. "I do not do relationships and I'm not about to start now. Not with a…" I paused, thinking of a polite way to describe him. "I am not your first set of training wheels for a gay relationship. You're going to find yourself some other guy for that. Now, I'm not saying I wouldn't oblige if you fancied a helping hand—a few tugs, or sucks, or even if you fancied sampling the full fuck. All those, I'd be happy to oblige, but as for a relationship, the answer is no." I folded my arms.

He tried to persuade me otherwise, said he was a good boyfriend, said he'd heard so from his ex-girlfriends, said he was all in for this with me, said he knew I felt something like he did, and how could I walk away from that. But I said nothing, I simply shook my head and kept my arms crossed.

We walked back to Liverpool Street station in silence. He tried to hold my hand but I didn't let him, pushing it away and making sure I was walking at least a foot from him. *Bloody holding hands. What next? Picking out curtains? Who does he think I am? Wait till I tell Bjorn. He'll laugh his head off at all this.*

I waved goodbye to Troy as I walked through the ticket barriers and then onto the escalator that took me on the Tube back home. I sat with my arms folded for the whole journey home, pleased with my decision, knowing the people that mattered would agree it was the right one.

CHAPTER 11

Troy

I WATCHED JULIAN DISAPPEAR down the escalator towards the crowds pushing into one another to get on the red line. *Julian said he lived on the red line. Or was it the brown line? It was a main station, one of the ones I'd heard of, definitely. Named after something, it was. A bear. Oh, I remember. Paddington.*

I paused by the Tube map trying to find where Paddington was—on the brown and pink lines too. I counted the number of stops from Liverpool Street to get him back home in Paddington and grabbed myself a Tube map from the ticket office window; maybe I'd need it later. No matter how many times I recounted the stops between here and Paddington, I still had an erection that refused to go away, and a head full of questions.

Society said I'd get a girlfriend, sleep with her, get pissed with my mates, carry on, have a kid with her. But I didn't want to do any of that, and I didn't know how to do what I really wanted.

CHAPTER 12

Julian

ANGIE AND I were at a coffee shop near our flat, discussing my date-but-not-a-date with Troy straight-but-not-straight the St John Ambulance worker.

Angie said, licking the foam off her coffee, "Isn't this some kind of fantasy for you? Luring the straight man over to the dark side?"

I looked at her from the side of my eyes. "Dark side? What do you think this is, the 1960s?"

She playfully slapped my arm. "Not even a little bit of a fantasy? A teensy weensy bit of one?"

"Troy is messy. He doesn't know what he wants. He's having a mid-life crisis, and he wants me for all the things I'm not—not a woman, not wanting to have a baby."

"Sounds as if you've got it all worked out. Why are you asking me what I think?" She stared out the window, stirring her coffee slowly.

"Because I'm not one hundred percent sure what I think."

"Tell me more."

"I don't want a relationship—never have done. Why would I change now? And I especially don't want a relationship with a bi-curious man who's only after me because I've not got a, you know. A pair of tits."

"What does this hunky rescuer man look like? Any pictures?"

I pulled out my phone and flicked through until I reached some pictures I'd taken during the date-not-a-date in the pub.

A few I'd taken from behind as he'd strode ahead, and a few I'd snapped while he was leaning on the bar buying drinks.

Angie took my phone from me and studied them carefully, pinching to zoom and scrolling between the pictures. Finally, she said, "If you don't want him, can I have him?"

I took my phone off her. "He's not something you can have. He's not a cat up for adoption, or a second-hand car. He's a person with feelings, and he's going through a big change in his life. He told me about his jumbled-up feelings for the gender of who he's attracted to, actually."

"So why aren't you treating him like a person?"

I put my hands in the air. "I'm not having a relationship. I don't want one. Imagine going out with him—he'd be all questions about who was the man and who was the woman in a gay relationship." I shuddered at the thought, based on some terribly tedious conversations I'd had with straight curious men over the years.

"How'd you know that? He might be the best boyfriend you could wish for. He might be a kind, considerate lover and a loving partner. If you don't give him a chance, you'll never know."

"Kind, considerate lover and loving partner. No, thank you. I'm not some heroine in a rom com. I want a man to be a man. I want an equal partner in a relationship. I want someone who can carry me upstairs so we can fuck each other ragged and then throw me around a bit more afterwards."

"Not that you've been thinking about it or anything?"

"Only in passing."

As I thought about this for a moment, we said nothing, only observing the other people in the café.

"Are you happy as you are?" she asked. "With the arrangement with Bjorn, and all the rest?"

"I'm not unhappy with it, if that's what you mean." I pursed my lips and crossed my legs.

"That's not what I asked. Don't you at least want to try and see what a relationship would be like?"

"No. Besides, if I did, I'd give it a go with Bjorn probably. At least he's something of a known quantity. Unlike Troy—God alone knows what I'd be letting myself in for with him."

"Judging by that arse and those thighs, I think I could tell you some of what you'd be letting yourself in for. I could easily imagine those thighs wrapped round my waist. Or yours for that matter." Angie smirked, indicated she'd finished her drink and asked if we were staying for another.

We left and walked along the canals of Little Venice, pausing under a tree to sit on a bench, watching a couple on their narrow boat as they hung out the washing and then ate sandwiches at the table and chairs at the back of the boat.

Angie said, "Why are you so against a relationship? What is it that scares you so much?"

"I'm not scared! No fucking way. Not scared at all. I don't know what makes you say that. When did I say I was scared? Why would I be scared of a relationship after the things I've done? Dark rooms in Mykonos, orgies in Barcelona, waking up with a tramp sucking me off on a bench... Nothing scares me. Especially not a relationship. Ridiculous." I shook my head. "Never heard anything so ridiculous. Scared."

"Maybe this is the universe's way of saying, now you've got to this age, it's time for a relationship—time to give one a try."

"You know I don't believe in all that fate and destiny crap. Life's what you make it, always has been, always will be."

"Life's thrown into your lap—or you into his lap—your very own hunky St John Ambulance man, who's telling you he's batting for your team, and not only that he likes you but that he can't stop thinking about you and wants to go out with you. You couldn't make this shit up."

"I don't want to be those people." I pointed to the elderly couple on the boat pouring tea together and eating in silence. "That's what a relationship does to you."

"Now we get to the truth. You *are* scared."

"I am not scared. If you say that again, I'm leaving you here and getting the Tube home."

She put her hands up in a defensive motion. "OK, not scared. Received and understood." She stared at the man and woman on the boat. "What's so bad about them? They look happy enough, don't they? Silent contentment. That's not just a relationship, that's fifty years of a relationship, right there."

"I don't want to end up on a boat, wearing slippers with some guy making me tea. I might as well throw myself in the canal now if that's what's in store for me. I am not that person."

"I think you're getting a few decades ahead of yourself. What would Bjorn say? How come he's not got a boyfriend?"

I thought back to a conversation I'd had with Bjorn towards the end of the last Sallie tour of America we'd done together. He'd been a bit drunk on red wine—always a precursor to emotional spillages, I'd noticed. "He said when he'd been with other guys briefly, he wanted to be with them and only them. They suggested an open relationship, and he'd just gone along with it because he thought that's what gay guys did."

"Didn't he want that?" Angie asked.

I shook my head. "He cried about it, actually—red wine's got a lot to answer for—said with one of his exes, finding the extra person for the threesome took over their relationship, so that's all they had in common in the end. Another guy he'd been with was shagging left, right and centre, and Bjorn could have done too, but all he wanted was to be with the other guy. Smelling the trade on his boyfriend and not taking advantage of the openness from his side, Bjorn ended up begrudging the boyfriend. Time and time again, slightly different story but the same outcome."

"Why didn't he say he didn't want to be open when it came up with these guys? Bjorn doesn't strike me as someone who lets himself be walked all over."

"Every time he thought it would be different. And it *was* slightly different—a different boyfriend, a different arrangement, different rules to stick to—but basically, it was always the same. He worried if he said no, the guy would go and do it anyway behind his back, so it was better to have it in the open."

"What did he really want?"

"I got that out of him eventually—some tears and more red wine later. He said, laughing a bit, he wanted a normal relationship, like most straight people have—just two people, that's all."

"And because he couldn't get that, he stuck with your little arrangement."

"Suits us both well. We're there for each other when we need to scratch that itch, and when we want someone else, that option's there too."

"And you're besties."

I shrugged. "Suppose so."

"Come on, you are."

"Yeah, we are."

"What does Bjorn have to say about Troy?"

I told her about his words of caution and both our experiences of being messed about by straight men.

"So, basically, you don't want to be hurt?"

"No, that's not it at all. I don't want to be in a relationship, to get old before my time. To get too comfortable with someone."

"In case you lose him?"

"No. Maybe. No."

"Come on, let's go home," Angie said, and we set off along the canal, our arms looped together. "Can I ask you one more question about Troy?"

"One more?" I asked, with a smile.

"Do you like him?"

"Like him, like him, or like him, like him?" I asked, not even making sense to myself, really.

"Is he a nice man?" she asked.

"He is," I replied.

"Then why don't you help him get through the maze of becoming gay? As a friend."

"There are worse things I could do, I suppose."

And with that, we continued walking in silence all the way along the canals through North Kensington and eventually back to Paddington where we arrived home and both went to our own bedrooms.

CHAPTER 13

Troy

Dear Dave,

I went for a drink with this Julian guy—the one I couldn't stop thinking about. Think I made a bit of a tit of myself, really, telling him how I feel. What does it mean? All I know is I want to see him again. I enjoy being around him. When he sat next to me in the pub, his leg pressing against mine, I wanted to hold him, to squeeze him tight. He kissed me goodbye at the station and disappeared, and all I could think about was him for the whole train journey home.

I might have told the taxi driver about my evening too, when I got back to the station. Yeah, I was definitely drunk. Taxi driver didn't seem arsed I was talking about some bloke I'd met in London. Maybe people don't care about that sort of thing anymore. Maybe people just want you to get on with your life.

I got home, made myself three rounds of toast with loads of butter and ate them in the kitchen with a can of beer. I felt like I was eighteen again, when anything is possible. I went to my room and lay on my back thinking about Julian, and I did something I've never done before—well, not in quite the same way. I've had a wank before, of course I have, but not while I've been thinking about a man. Not since that time in the woods.

I imagined Julian's hands on me, on my body. He looks like he's pretty smooth—didn't see much hair, which I like. I've decided I like smooth men.

There, I said it, I like smooth men's bodies.

I lay on my back imagining his body, imagining if the hair around his belly button was the same colour as the hair on his head, and the light hairs on the backs of his hands. In my mind, it was a bit darker, a bit more wiry. I have never felt so fucking turned on in my life—more than when I went to the strip club in Amsterdam on that stag do; more than when Freya used to wear the underwear I said I liked her in and take it off slowly. Just the thought of Julian's imaginary hair down there made me as stiff as a board.

That was how I woke up the next morning, my trousers and pants round my ankles, my cock in my hand and my stomach covered in dried spunk. As I remembered why I was lying there, I felt sick to my stomach. I thought I'd managed to hide this. Since eighteen, I'd hidden it all away, thought I'd got over it, that it wasn't part of me.

Why has it come back to me now? Why this time? Why this man? How am I meant to tell everyone, now, after forty years, and girlfriends, that I like men—men's belly button hair and men's smooth bodies?

Who can I tell about this except you? Who can I explain it to when I can't explain it to myself?

I wonder if it's just Julian, or if it's all men?

I feel like I'm eighteen again, but then I remember I'm forty and think about how many years I've wasted living the wrong life, living a lie.

I think I've scared him off. Too much. Too soon. But I don't know how I'm going to do this without his help. Even if he doesn't want to be with me, I need him in my life somehow. I need to work out how to do that. But really I want him to be with me.

CHAPTER 14

Julian

B ACKSTAGE, A FEW weeks later, I was staring at myself in the mirror, wondering what to do.

Bjorn stood next to me, checking out his exposed skin in the blue feathery outfit he wore. "Can you glitter me up?" He gestured to his back. "Sallie said we're to cover every exposed inch of flesh with as much glitter as possible. As if the blue feathers and glittery little hot pants aren't enough, but who are we to argue?" He rolled his eyes and held out a container of glitter.

"Turn around." As I started to spread the glittery lotion over his broad shoulders, my mind wandered to the possibilities after the show and whether I should join him in his hotel room.

"You are quiet. What is wrong?" Bjorn asked, tensing his bum cheeks so they made a smile in the rear of his blue sequinned hot pants. "Smile, will you? I am."

"I'm tired. It's nothing," I replied. I continued rubbing in the glitter, then squeezed Bjorn's bum. "Have you adjusted these? Only, they look tighter than they were before."

Bjorn turned to face me, the front of his hot pants as tight as the back, with an attractive bulge in the shiny sequins. "I am trying some new underwear. They are like a Wonderbra for the arse. They push it up and together. And the front, it is the same. Worth it, I think?"

"Very impressive. What's it in aid of?"

"Did I tell you about the follower on Twitter who messaged me? He said he was at the front when we were in Stockholm. Said he wanted to unwrap my package. I wanted to give him more of a package to unwrap." He smirked.

"Is he here tonight?"

Bjorn shrugged. "He said he would be. We have been in touch."

"Pictures?" I caught his eyes through the mirror.

"A few." He met my gaze, then looked away.

"Be careful. That's a few clicks away from a stalker. He could be anyone."

"I'm a big boy. I can look after myself." He did a twirl in front of the mirror. "I am done now. How is it? Am I covered?"

"Head to toe."

"Fucking fabulous. Besides, this is only a bit of fun. I wanted to tease him. If he is here. I will not do anything. Not tonight. Not with him. Maybe a drink. Something to eat... But I could do with something to unwind. Someone. My room afterwards?"

It had been a while since I'd got any action. My head had been all over the place since Troy's little confession, and part of me was flattered that he liked me in that way. Part of me was terrified what it meant. The rest of me just wanted to get my rocks off, which was what Bjorn's and my arrangement was meant for. "Sounds good." I smiled at him.

"I have some new toys we could try. Man in the shop said it was just what I would enjoy."

As Bjorn gave me the lurid details of these new toys he'd bought—and conveniently brought on tour with him...and my interest was pricked...and my cock started to respond—my phone rang.

It was Troy. He didn't wait for me to say hello, or ask how I was, he just started with, "When can we see each other again? I've been thinking about it, and I have to see you. Even if it's just as friends. I think I'm shit at this whole gay thing. I need someone to sort of show me around it. There, I said it. Got it out in the open. That's my cards on the table, where do you stand?"

"I'm about to go on stage actually, but thanks for asking."

Bjorn mouthed 'Troy' at me, and I nodded.

To Troy, I said, "I told you I don't date. I haven't dated and I won't date. But I'm happy to be friends. No harm in that." I thought of Bjorn and my friendship and briefly wondered if Troy and I could have something similar but quickly brushed that thought aside and concentrated on the mid-life crisis in hand. "Friends. Take it or leave it."

"I'll take it," he replied instantly.

"I'm only a few years off my own mid-life crisis, so helping you with yours can be a dry run. Help me prepare for my own."

"What makes you think that's what this is?" He sounded genuinely hurt and confused.

"Forty years old. Split up with your girlfriend. Meet me and I'm the answer to your now-gay prayers. Honey, all you need is a sports car and you've got the whole nine yards."

Troy was silent on the end of the line.

Maybe that was a bit far. "Sorry."

"It's fine. I'm just getting used to your style of banter. If this is my mid-life crisis, I'm taking part in it. I'm owning it. I am my mid-life crisis. At least it's something I want, not something I'm being dragged through by someone else, like the rest of my life has been."

"Sorry," I said again. I really had gone too far. "I'm with you."

"Then I'm with you too," he replied and then hung up as suddenly as he'd started the call.

The stage manager poked his head around the door. "Five minutes, everyone. Julian, make sure you're glittered up, special request from Sallie. Bjorn, give him a hand, will you? And keep it clean—five minutes, all right?" With a wink he was gone.

Bjorn covered his hands in the glittery substance, turned me away from him and started to rub it into my back and shoulders. "Do not worry if you do not want to come to my room afterwards. I will not be offended. I'm sure the enhancing underwear will work wonders. Someone in the audience, they are bound to catch my eye."

"What you chatting about now?"

"That phone call."

The stage manager threw open the doors and told us to take our places, bustling us out of the room into the stage wings where we waited for Sallie to descend in a human-sized birdcage, dressed as a yellow canary, wings and beak and everything, singing one of her newest ballads about finding the love of her dreams and singing to him from across the stars.

During the whole set, whenever Bjorn caught my gaze, he shook his head slightly and rolled his eyes.

***

Later that night, after a few hours in the hotel bar, drinks courtesy of Sallie and a few bowls of peanuts courtesy of the hotel, I found myself in Bjorn's room, holding a bottle of cava we'd taken up from the bar and offering to pour us two more glasses.

Bjorn lay on the white sofa, all of his outfit long since removed, except the very tight, very shiny, very sequinned blue hot pants. His chest was covered in blue glitter from where one of the other dancers had smeared it from his back onto his front, and he lay with his head propped up on a pillow and his arms above his head. He had his eyes closed and his lips pursed as if he was kissing an imaginary someone.

"Oi, I said, any more fizz? And never mind pouting. Who you kissing in your mind?"

"He didn't come tonight. He messaged me he was ill and he asked me please can I send him the hot pants I had told him about."

"Wardrobe will kill you, then make you buy another pair, then kill you again."

He waved theatrically in the air. "This, I know. I do not think he ever was here. I think he just saw me on Twitter and he said he was here. And there they go, another one passes by." He patted the sofa next to him and slid down so his head was level with his body and his legs hung over the arms of the sofa. He pointed at his chin. "Take off your clothes and sit here."

As much as normally the prospect of sitting on Bjorn's face would have appealed because, without going into too much detail, he had a long tongue and an adept technique that had on occasions made me come without even touching my cock, tonight, I wasn't in the mood. I kept my clothes on and sat next to him.

He licked his lips. "What is wrong? You are here. I am here. We both know why this is."

"Do you mind if tonight, we don't?"

He sat up, both eyes open and a quizzical look on his face. "I think I am right. This is the phone call earlier, no?"

"Better I stay just friends with him, isn't it?" I paused, staring into Bjorn's eyes. "Simpler."

"Fuck simpler. Who wants simpler? If I had a man like that telling me he liked me, I'd stick my head up his arse and wear him like a hat. I would lock him in my house and show him some good proper gay sex. Show him what he missed all these years. But if you think it is simpler to be friends, you go ahead."

"Oh."

"You fancy him?"

"A bit." I bit my lip.

"OK, if it's nothing, then come here and you sit on my face. We can have a good sexy time together like we usually do. Nothing more to it."

I shook my head. "A bit. I fancy him a bit."

"Bollocks! You told me he gave you a stiffy in the treatment room. I've seen the photos. He's fucking gorgeous. Here is an idea—how about you give it a go."

"I can't."

"Can't or won't?" Bjorn was stroking my arm now.

"Troy is what I always avoid. He's the sort of man who takes the piss out of guys like us. He's on the rebound. He wants me because I'm not a woman."

"But he still wants you. And guys like us? Speak for yourself. We are individuals, and so is he. What is the worst that can happen?"

I thought about the old couple on the boat making tea together, and my heart froze.

"If you sleep with him and it does not work out, you can still be friends. Look at us! And then, you will have fucking well slept with him. He's this big man opportunity of sex and you are ignoring it. That is against some gay rules or something."

"I don't know how to do a relationship."

"No one does. You make it up as you go along. Now, are we done with this? We've got to check out in four hours. Do you want to unwind with me in the four-poster bed? Or do I have to take a cold shower?"

I kissed him and thanked him, climbed out of my clothes and walked to his bed a few steps from the sofa.

Bjorn climbed in bed behind me, spooning me. Nothing to separate our bodies, not even his spangly hot pants, but after a quick kiss and him saying, "Do not mention it," we fell asleep exactly like that.

***

The next morning, we showered separately, walking around the hotel room naked as I collected my things and he packed his into a suitcase. After all the stuff Bjorn and I had done in bed together, seeing each other naked was nothing. And he was fantastically uninhibited physically and sexually, which, after knowing him so long, had rubbed off on me.

I moved to the door and told him I'd meet him in the tour bus shortly.

He kissed my cheek. "It was fun while it lasted. Go. Be happy. Be with him. And I am always here if you need me—for nights like before, or nights like last night."

CHAPTER 15

Troy

I WAS DOING THE first aid for some girl band. They'd recently reformed, having realised they were from the nineties and so officially retro, and clearly all needed the money—they even sang some stuff I recognised. Anyway, I was backstage, chatting to some of the dancers—all male, and all gay, it seemed.

There was a group of us around the back of the stage chatting and sipping bottles of water. "What do you do in the week when you're not all green-jumpsuited up?" one of the guys said, stroking my arm.

"I'm a gardener," I replied.

They all laughed at that for some reason. I wasn't sure why.

"I've been called an uphill gardener," another said, laughing with the other dancers.

"I do this because it's what I want to do. I want to work as an ambulance paramedic. But it takes a while to do the training. And I've got to earn a living."

"He does work hard, doesn't he, this one?" said the first guy, who'd now moved on to squeezing my biceps. "What other concerts have you done?"

"Sallie. When she was in London. I was backstage there."

"At the O2?" he asked, mouth open.

I nodded.

They asked what she was like—was she like she seemed on the telly? Was she really that short? Had she had any work done?

I explained how I'd found her very natural and kind and down-to-earth.

"Not like that American some of us worked for last season. Fucking nightmare. He was an ex-talent-show winner and thought he'd invented singing. Went over the dance moves and changed them at the last minute. Chucked off the lighting guy to replace him with someone new. Fired the stage manager because she hadn't done her roots in a while."

They laughed. I laughed.

When there was a silence in the chat, one of the guys said, "What does your girlfriend think of you doing this job? Does she like you in the uniform? I know I would. If my boyfriend was in uniform, I'd not be able to get enough of it, when he got home." He winked at the others. "If you know what I mean."

Another guy said, "We know exactly what you mean. It's what you always mean. You're scaring this poor man. Look at you, draping yourself all over him." He removed his friend's arms from around my neck.

And then, because I'd not done this before, and now seemed as good a time as any to try it out for size, I said, "I don't have a girlfriend."

"Poor man."

"I'm gay, man." The words hung in the air between us. I held my breath, expecting an announcement from the public address system that I'd come out to these people, or for them to hand me a welcome-to-the-club card or something.

"I knew it," said one of the men, laughing.

"There's a lot of it about," added another.

"They walk amongst us," said a third.

"A gardener and a first-aider. And one of us. All in the one package." He eyed up my green jumpsuit uniform. "Don't suppose you're looking for a boyfriend, are you?"

"I don't have one. But I might." I paused, struggling to explain Julian, me, and coming out so late. "It's complicated."

"That's our favourite sort of story," he replied. "Come with us, and tell us all about it."

Another guy interrupted, "But first, I want to see how your hips swing. Come on, copy us. If this guy's a dancer, you'd better learn to get your dance on, show him you have rhythm. Rhythm on the dance floor shows rhythm in the bedroom. Trust me."

They went on stage to do their thing, and I returned to the first-aid area where I treated a twenty-something woman for dehydration, a nineteen-year-old man with a grazed knee from when he'd fallen over, and a middle-aged woman who'd forgotten her anti-anxiety tablets and had a panic attack in the crowd.

As I was tidying the equipment away and getting ready to make my way home, I felt a tap on my shoulder. I turned to see a group of guys in jeans and T-shirts, broad smiles on their faces. It took me a while to realise they were the dancers from earlier because now they looked like normal guys in their twenties, as opposed to the leather-trussed packages they'd appeared before going on stage.

"Coming? There's an afterparty, guest list only. And guess who got us all on the guest list?"

I shrugged, wondering if it would be better for me to make my excuses and go home.

"Nadia Marshall."

This name meant nothing to me. I shrugged again and threw in a yawn for good measure. "It's been a long day and I've got to be up early tomorrow. And I was up early today, so—"

Before I could say any more, I was being swept along in the middle of the group, one of them explaining the woman was one of the girl band who'd been playing. She was married to a Premier League footballer who I had heard of, actually.

There was a fire escape in a back alley and a door hidden behind it which led to a club that was like an advert for a Club 18-30 holiday: large bowls of blue liquid which we all shared through straws; men in shorts dancing in cages; women in bikinis dancing in boxes suspended above the dance floor; a shiny silver bar with a mirror behind it and rows and rows of colourful drinks.

"We'll start from the left side, and work our way to the right. And you can start at the beginning..."

The other dancers finished the line from the well-known musical song about how that was the best place to start.

He continued, "And you can tell us all about this dancer. Name, age, shoe size, eye colour. I don't want you to miss out any details." He eyed up the barman who started making another bowl of drink, this time bright red.

I did as asked and told them as much as I knew about Julian. After the red drink in a bowl, we had a green one, and I found myself receiving lessons on how to dance from two of the men. One stood behind me, resting his hands on my hips and telling me to feel the music, to embrace it with my body. "That'll do for now," he finished with before disappearing into the crowd of dancing people.

The man who'd first spoken to me backstage sat next to me now. He rested his head on his hand and his elbow on the table. He pointed at me, emphasising every word with a stab of the finger. "This Julian... Well-preserved thirty-something. Blond. Blue eyes. Always clean-shaven. Couldn't grow a beard if he tried?"

I nodded.

He snapped his fingers. "I know him. I knew him. He used to dance with this girl band—until he disappeared and started working for Sallie." He pursed his lips.

"He always wanted to work for her. She's lovely to work for."

"Yeah, yeah, down-to-earth, friendly, hasn't had any work done. I know, I've heard it all before." He paused, pushed the half-empty fish bowl of aquamarine liquid towards me. "Want some?"

I waved it away. I wasn't used to drinking spirits, not in this sort of quantity, anyway. Keeping up with rounds of beers after a football match had nothing on this lot.

"Please yourself." He sipped from the straw, closing his eyes. "Julian. Very popular man." He opened his eyes then raised his eyebrows.

"Why? Were you seeing him?" I asked.

"It was complicated." He paused, laughing to himself. "Or very simple, I suppose." More laughing.

I banged my fist on the table. "What do you mean?"

"He was a popular member of the dancing company. Liked to spread himself around. Always said yes. Never one to turn down a party. Of whatever kind."

I was biting my lip now, not sure why, but I wanted to say something, not ask more questions but to come to Julian's rescue with this man who claimed to know him yet didn't really know him at all. "Why don't you shut up?"

"Meow. Who's rattled your cage? It's only a joke."

"I love him," I replied.

"You and me both, love." He laughed to himself.

"No, I really love him."

"You said it was complicated. Best you go and tell him. Leave me here with my fish bowl."

I swiftly left the club, only briefly catching the eye of one of the other dancers. As I walked from the back street to a main road and eventually to a taxi rank, I regretted leaving without saying goodbye to the guys. In the main, they'd been friendly, interested and interesting to me, and they'd helped me work out where I really stood with Julian. Except the last guy. His jokiness about Julian's past and how it hadn't meant anything made me want to punch him. Not that I ever would have done. It was something about how smug he'd been, telling me he'd slept with Julian without actually telling me, and especially after I'd shared that I'd not gone that far with Julian yet.

Jealousy? Envy? Frustration? Maybe a bit of all three. If not, it was definitely there or thereabouts. I'd never felt like that about any girlfriend, not even after years together. I used to laugh it off when they introduced me to their exes—why care about that? The dancer wasn't even an ex of Julian's. And Julian had been honest about his colourful past with me, so why, when it was being described to me by someone else, had I reacted like that?

***

After a few days of these thoughts swirling around my head, not knowing what else to do—certainly knowing I couldn't contact any of the dancers again after embarrassing myself so much, despite their friendly offers of help—I sent Julian an email. I say 'sent'—it stayed in drafts for a week, with me changing words and phrases here and there, forgetting about it, then coming back to it most evenings after work. I even managed to get a bit of advice from Olive at work and include that too.

"Tell your friend to tell the girlfriend what he feels. What he's worried about. Better than keeping it in. You'll feel better," she had said one evening after everyone else had left the kitchen and it was only us two left.

"My friend?" I repeated.

"Your friend. With the girlfriend trouble," she replied.

***

Hello Julian—

Even that took a lot of consideration—was 'Dear' too formal? Was 'Hi' too chatty? How about just 'Julian'? In the end, I settled on the above.

I am not a safe bet. I am a mess. Yes, I am on the rebound. From women. All women. And yes, I like you because you're not a woman.

But, I can't stop thinking about you. I nearly punched a gay guy who was talking about you. Don't know why. It was like I was defending your honour or something. I don't do that. I've never defended someone's honour before. I barely care about my own honour.

Anyway, enough about honour. I know you don't need me defending yours—I know yours probably disappeared years ago, lol!

I felt closer to you that night, in your changing room, just talking and being together, than the whole seven years with Freya, my ex.

Fuck. That makes me a fucking horrible person, doesn't it? Wasting her life for all that time? Pretending I was with her when I wasn't really. Stopping her getting with another guy so she could have the life she wanted with me. The life I never really wanted, but it's taken me all this time to realise what I wanted.

What a fucking idiot I am. What a selfish idiot.

I know it's my life, and it's for me to live it, but I wasted Freya's and other's lives because I didn't know who I was. What an idiot.

And here's something to make you laugh. I bet you and your mates will shit yourself at this—I'm still going to say it because I can't talk about it 'cos that's even worse, and I have to tell you—I am terrified about the sex.

Go on, laugh at me.

I bet you are now. Passing this around your friends. Putting it on Facebook.

I don't care, because if you are, then it's another thing that won't kill me and will make me stronger. Even if we're not friends, or anything more, I will find others who will be friends with me.

Where was I? The sex. Scared shitless. How does it work? What's it like? How do you know who does which part? What if I'm really bad at it? I've been told I was a pretty good shag by the women I've slept with, but that's all different. What if I'm a terrible gay shag?

I know we said we'd give being friends a try, and if that's what you're offering, I'll take it. You said you and your friend Bjorn talk about all the sex, and so I hope this is what gay friends talk to each other about.

Yours, confused, Troy

***

I deleted the kisses, then put them back, then deleted them again. I'd sent an odd text ending with a kiss, or not, because that's what you do when you're with someone, isn't it? But I wasn't with Julian.

I added some brackets with hugs written inside—I'd seen people do it on Facebook—then decided it was a bit over the top and not really me.

I debated a smiley face, but when I read through what I'd written, I realised it wasn't a very smiley email, so deleted that too.

Never before had I spent so long writing such a short email to anyone. Before, I didn't fear sex—I didn't enjoy it, but I thought it was like so much of life: something to be endured, to be got through—so there wasn't much to write about then. Before, I didn't feel anything, so I didn't write about how I felt.

CHAPTER 16

Julian

I RE-READ HIS EMAIL. At first, I'd found it quite funny—the outpouring of the heart of a confused new gay man—then when Angie read it, she said, "Don't laugh. He's confused. He's opened his heart to you and you're laughing." She shook her head and tutted loudly, folding her arms across her chest.

"Not funny. Understood."

"This, you know. Because you're not a cruel person. What does Bjorn think?"

"I've laid off asking him about it for a while." I told her about the night of the almost fuck buddies and how we'd slept together but hadn't done anything.

"You and Bjorn?"

"Yes."

"After a show, neither of you pulled, and you went to his room with champagne and got drunk and you didn't fool around?"

"Nope."

"But that's what you two do. That's your thing. It's what you are together. Julian and Bjorn, fuck buddies and best friends."

"We're still friends. I've told him everything since we met. We've seen each other naked hundreds of times. If I close my eyes, I could describe to you his—"

"No, thank you very much. So why the change?" Angie asked.

"I didn't want to, not with him, not when I was still thinking about this Troy and how much he wanted me. Someone wanting you, like a proper love job—it's pretty good for the ego."

"This new you isn't as nice as the old you. What have you done to the old Julian?"

"He's stopped getting his regular supply of sex with anyone and everyone, and he's trying to make sense of a straight man's email." I sighed.

"He is not straight. He's talking about the sex, and the worries about all the gay sex. Does that sound like a straight man to you?"

"Well, now you come to mention it…"

"For fuck's sake, make a decision, will you?" Throwing her hands in the air in despair, she went on, "I'm flying to Brisbane tomorrow. If, when I get home next week, you're still faffing about like this, I'm bringing in Bjorn to clear your mind."

"You always say sex is sex, and love is love. So why am I having the big hang-up this time?" I shook my head.

"Surely, if there's anyone who can ease Troy gently into the new world of gay sex, it's you. I mean, you're so experienced… Maybe throw in Bjorn for good luck?"

"He's said he wants to leave me to it. With Troy, just me and Troy."

"Bjorn said that? He's passing up a chance with an ex-straight man with that body and a St John Ambulance uniform? Who killed Bjorn and replaced him with this robot? I don't know what's up with you guys, but it's shaking my world view. It's frying my mind."

"He didn't say that so much, but he said he always wanted a relationship and wanted to leave me to it with this one. Hence the night of no sex." I paused for a moment, attempting to collect my thoughts and feelings into some semblance of making sense. "I've no problem with the sex with Troy. None at all. In fact, I've been thinking about it quite a bit since I've not seen Bjorn so much."

"Well, then." Angie clapped her hands. "At fucking last, a resolution. A decision. Halle-bloody-lujah!"

"The sex is the easy part. It's the part I've stuck with since I was eighteen. It's the bit I know inside out, upside down and back to front. Especially upside down and back to front."

"All right, no need to boast. So what's stopping you? If you fuck and that's it, it's no different from you and Bjorn—well, how you and he were. What's to lose? You fuck, you stop fucking, you're friends. That's what gay guys are best at, you always say. That's the beauty of it."

I sighed. "You may well have to kill me when you're back from Brisbane. It's all the mess around the sex I'm worried about. That's the difficult stuff I've not done before. I never wanted a relationship and I don't want one now." Or did I?

"You've got him spilling his heart out to you in an email. That takes guts. You could do anything with it, put it on the internet, send it to your whole address book, anything. Vulnerability, that's what it shows."

"Does it? Really? Or does it show he's confused and I was in his line of sight when he realised he batted for the other team?"

"People change. Do you want to be Bjorn's fuck buddy until you're in your sixties? Are you going to be swiping left through hookup apps and chatting to guys in bars when you're collecting your pension?"

I put my hands on my hips and pouted. Because, although I'd not thought of it in such an extreme way before, I believed it was my right to do that if I wanted, right up to my dying day. "If I want to, yes," I said.

"Give it a go with this Troy, and if it turns to shit, go back to fucking and going. They're not going to throw you out of the club."

"What club?" I frowned.

"The gay club. It was a joke. Look, what's the worst that can happen?"

"I lose my heart to a straight St John Ambulance paramedic and he goes back to his girlfriend."

"So get under someone else, and you'll bounce back."

"Not from something that's been a bit of a fantasy of mine for all these years. Meeting a straight man who I turn gay. My very own masc man."

"Bjorn's hardly as camp as Christmas."

"But I don't love Bjorn. Not in that way." As soon as it came out of my mouth, I knew that was the real problem. "I don't love Troy. I hardly know him. But I love the fact he wants a relationship with me, and that he's making me think about if I want one too. And he is fucking gorgeous. An arse that—"

"If that's how you feel, you have to give it a go. You can't start a relationship thinking it will end. You've got to go in all guns a-blazing, full on, believing you're running towards your happy-ever-after."

"All right." I put my hand up, really having had enough of all this sugary romance and love talk. "Enough of the rom com speech."

"Are we done here?"

"We're done." I'm done for. Fucking. Done. For. Hurtling towards the unknown, a mass of hurt and mess, just like I'd seen my friends experience as their relationships inevitably ended. Briefly I remembered Bjorn, lying flat on the sofa, ready for me to sit on his face, and I longed for how much simpler that was than what I was thinking about doing now.

Angie had left me alone, busy packing in her bedroom, occasionally reappearing to collect essentials from the flat and reminding me to put my duty-free requests on the list on the fridge door.

I texted Bjorn: *I think I'm going on a date. May need your relationship advice x*

He replied: *Basically, whatever I did with my exes do the opposite! Xx*

I replied: *missed you after work last week.*

Bjorn: *went home, picked up in Soho—twink to work out the frustrations on, was screaming so loud I had to gag him—back to mine afterwards. Watched a film alone.*
Me: *Always welcome to mine for film nights—only the films now I think!*
Bjorn: *sounds good xxx*
Me: *xxx*

***

It was as if my whole world was changing around me—my relationship with Angie, my film nights with Bjorn—all because of Troy. *Is this what people do when they're in a relationship? And I'm not even in one yet, not properly. Fuck knows how much more is going to change when it really starts.* But I decided it was better not to think about that for the time being.

CHAPTER 17

Troy

I HAD BEEN HANGING around the kitchen, trying to snatch bits of conversation with Olive for most of the afternoon. I'd watched her peeling and cutting, whisking and beating and putting a series of large metal dishes into and onto the Aga before continuing with more whisking and cutting, and then taking them out of the Aga…

"Haven't you got some bulbs want planting, young Troy?" she asked as she took a teaspoon of sauce from a bubbling pot.

"All planted. Can I help?" I pointed to a pile of carrots on the wooden worktop.

"That's what I've got Carley for. But she's not here today—flu, she reckons—I suppose you know that since you're in here. Never see you from one week to the next otherwise." She pointed to a chopping board and handed me a knife. "Get on with it. All them carrots and then the potatoes want peeling and cutting and parboiling. Think you can manage that?"

I started with the carrots. "I'll do these first, shall I?"

"What did you say to that Carley girl? I've never heard her talk about you since. You didn't have your way with her and send her packing, did you?"

I stared at a carrot, focusing all my mind on peeling it.

Olive clipped me round the head gently. "Oi, I asked you a question. What happened with you and Carley? I thought you were going to get on like a house on fire."

I peeled another carrot, concentrating equally as hard as on the previous one. *A house on fire—people running from the building, flames everywhere, fire engine drenching everything in water.* Maybe we had.

Another clip round the ear. "Are you deaf? I'm not talking to myself for my own health, you know. I get enough time to do that when I'm alone. Least you could do is answer me."

"She's very pretty. Very sweet. Lovely girl." I stopped peeling the carrot and noticed how like a penis it looked. *Is this what happens when you realise you're gay, you suddenly start seeing cocks everywhere?* "That was the problem."

"What, she was too pretty? Never heard anything so stupid in my life. She's not posh, no airs and graces, she's natural pretty, that's what I call it."

I turned my back to Olive and started to peel the next carrot, this time slowly. "That she's a girl. A woman."

"What you on about? What about your Freya, and the young girl you was with when you came here. Broke your heart when you split up with her, you said. And hers."

"Claire," I replied. "Mistakes. I've been making mistakes for my whole life, and now I'm not. No more mistakes with my life or anyone else's. No more women."

"Oh no, you can't go celibate. Not a big strong young lad like you. 'Snot right. I had another lad work here with me, before your time. He was celibate, he said. Wanted to take a vow of silence too, but I said I had no use for a vow of silence in my kitchen. Left to join a monastery in the end. Shame, 'cos he made the best meringues I've ever seen. Chewy on the inside and crisp and white on the outside. People used to come from all around just to see his pavlovas. Wonder if they eat pavlovas in a monastery, with the monks…" She stared out the window, resting both hands on the worktop in front of her. She wiped her brow with a tea towel dangling from the string around her apron. "What do you want to go and be celibate for? Pretty girl like that. I bet if you talked to her, she'd give you another chance."

"I'm not going celibate. No more women. But I'm not celibate. I am a gay man."

She slapped my arm playfully. "No you're not. Don't be so silly. Get on with the carrots and tell me what's really on your mind." She shook her head, tutting loudly.

"I am a gay man."

"You? But you've been with women your whole life. You play rugby for the village. I've seen you dance at the Christmas party, and you've got two left feet. You live in those flannel shirts and dirty jeans—even when you're not working. You can't be gay. Can you?"

I nodded. "Yes."

"Why now? Why so late? Does it mean I could become gay next week?" She sat at the table and wiped her eyes with her apron. "Sorry."

"What you apologising for?"

"I don't understand how you can become gay at your age. And I'm sorry for if I've said anything that's not quite right. Never assume, I'm always told by my friend Mavis. We watch that dancing programme together, and one week there was this man. Oh, he was gorgeous." She paused for a moment, her eyes showing her brain was working out the implications of that statement. "He was on one of these reality TV programmes, had a girlfriend, all blonde hair and teeth—her, not him. He had a big tall quiff just like Elvis, and a bushy beard and moustache, not like Elvis. She used to watch him play football—some local team, nothing much. Well, Mavis said, when I was saying how I wished I was thirty years younger or this lad was thirty years older, she said that he was on the other bus. You know what I mean? *The other bus.*"

I knew about the other bus. In fact, at that moment, I was probably collecting tickets for this so-called other bus. I nodded for her to continue.

"He was on one bus, with the girlfriend and the blonde hair and the teeth, and next thing, he's on the other bus. I said, 'Would he still be playing football?' and Mavis said she'd seen him in some magazine talking about it, with the other dancing competition contestants. There he was, bold as brass, dancing with this pretty Russian girl. Bloody hell, could he move. His hips during the rumba... So I suppose there's a lot of it about. It happens."

"It does."

"But love, are you sure?"

"I've never been as scared of anything in my life. Never felt like this before. Just went along with it—'cos it was what everyone expected me to do—but this? This means something to me, which is why I wanted to ask for your help."

She pointed to the carrots. "They're not going to peel themselves. Get them done, and when you start the potatoes, I'll show you how to parboil them and maybe then we can talk about whatever else you want to ask me about." She walked to the other side of the kitchen, took a deep breath, sprinkled flour onto a marble board and stirred something in a bowl.

After I'd finished the carrots, I started peeling the potatoes. Olive had stayed on her side of the kitchen, leaving me to mine and my carrots. Having peeled the potatoes, I sat next to them and waited.

After a few moments, I felt a hand on each shoulder. "They're too big for a start off. Cut 'em in half at least and put 'em in that saucepan." Her hands remained on my shoulders, stopping me from standing. "If you want me to say I saw it coming, you'll be waiting a long time. If you want me to say I'm not shocked, don't hold your breath. If you want me to say I understand it and tell me all about it, I'm sorry, you're out of luck there too—for the moment."

I started to stand but she held me down.

"But I will say this. I think you're the bravest man I've seen in a long time. I might not understand it, but if you're happy, I'm happy for you. How's that for a starter? I'm sure the rest will come with time, or not, we'll see, eh?"

I remained seated.

She hugged me from behind and kissed my cheek. "I know you're not my son, but you might as well be, which is why this is hard for me. But it's only because I care for you. I care for you a lot more than an old cook should care for a gardener thirty years younger than her. Now those tatties are on, how about you ask me what you're wanting to ask me." She walked slowly to the Aga, pulled up a chair and sat, her arms folded across her chest.

"I have a date. Only I don't want to scare him off. By being too full on."

"What's her...I mean his name, love?"

"Julian."

"Tell me what he does and where you met him—what he's like—and let's see if we can work something out. It's been many long years since I went on a date, but I can tell you what's unattractive and sure to scare someone off." She pulled up a chair next to hers in front of the Aga and patted it for me to join her.

"Yes?"

"Being fake. Pretending to laugh at everything he says, to agree with everything he says, saying all his jokes and stories are the funniest you've heard. All that gets boring. No one's that funny. Some jokes, some stories, OK, but not all of 'em. And I'll tell you what it shows too, which isn't attractive either—desperation."

"What if he *is* that funny?"

"Be yourself. Be your natural, kind, attentive, interested self. You can make anything seem interesting if you describe it right and show your passion to the other person. I bet you weren't that interested in Sallie or dancing at first, were you?"

"Not really my scene. But Julian, he made me want to know more."

She stared into my eyes. "That's good."

"That's what I thought."

"Not that. I mean how your eyes light up when you say his name. That's some special kind of magic is that."

"What about flowers or chocolates? Should I buy him some?"

"Don't ask me, love. Who knows what a man buys a man for a first date? Keep it simple and personal. Save the big gestures for later. Don't peak too early."

"What should I wear? I'm not very good with clothes—always in a uniform, or jeans and checked shirts."

"Which are your own uniform I suppose. Just stay as yourself, that's all I think you need to remember."

"And my hair?" I asked, optimistically.

"Gay, straight, bi, whatever else there is, whatever you do, just be handsome. Be the best you that you can be."

"Can you help me?"

"Isn't this helping?" she asked.

"I mean shopping, clothes, haircut…everything. I don't have a clue what to do." And so, we were off.

***

Olive borrowed her son's *GQ* magazine for tips, took me to a barber's for my haircut and to some little shops off the beaten track in Chelmsford's back streets where the assistants brought you clothes from mysterious unseen areas of the shop and told you if they suited you or not.

And that was how, now, I found myself in a bar in Soho, wearing tight black jeans, a shirt that reminded me of my granny's wallpaper, a waistcoat, and a hairstyle like the one who stands nearest the camera in a boy band.

I leant against the white painted wall of the courtyard. One side led to the bar where I'd bought myself something brightly coloured in a long glass with a straw; the other side led out to the street. There was a balcony above me with groups of men staring down at me and laughing. Laughing at my ridiculous outfit and haircut, expecting me to be joined by three other similarly dressed men to practise our harmonies.

It was full of gays. Sorry, gay men. I knew I was a gay man too, but these seemed different, like they were all in on some shared joke, all laughing together. Groups of them stood around sipping drinks and taking it in turns to tell stories and laugh at the punchlines. In fairness, some of the punchlines were pretty amusing, or offensive, or both, but this was nothing like any straight pub I'd been to with tables and pints of beer and people talking quietly about mortgages and house prices and their kids. *I am not one of these people, so what the fuck am I doing here?*

Just as I was checking my watch—realising Julian was ten minutes late, and wondering if it would be better for me, the gays of the world and Julian if I packed up my toys and stopped pretending to be something I wasn't—Julian appeared in front of me.

He looked similar to me—similar clothes at any rate, only they suited him. They *were* him. He held his hands to either side, shaking them slightly, like jazz hands.

I laughed nervously. What was I supposed to do?

He kissed my cheek, then the other one.

Not knowing what to do, I leant forward to do the same, but then realised we'd already kissed and now I looked wrong. No one else had done this when they'd arrived—I'd noticed a few arrivals and greetings while waiting for Julian. They had just kissed each other on the lips or hugged. None of this two kiss, two cheeks palava.

After a bit of chat about our journeys and the weather and if I'd been to this bar before—"No, not yet. Lively, isn't it?"—I asked what he wanted to drink and turned to walk inside.

Julian grabbed my shoulder. "You've got a drink, I'll go."

"But, I'm... It's me who... Don't you want me to go to the bar?" Freya never went to the bar. She always said it wasn't for her to do. She was modern in lots of ways, but on that she'd been very clear. Men go to the bar and women sit.

"Not at the moment, I don't. You're not my servant. I'll get myself one and whatever you're having." He left.

When he returned, sipping his drink and putting mine on a ledge behind us on the wall, he said, "What you drinking this shit for? They do beer, you know. It's in bottles, so it's not all organic, natural free range, but I'm sure it's still proper beer."

"Oh."

"Big fridges full of the stuff behind the bar. How'd you miss 'em?" Julian sipped his orange mixture through a straw, then bit the cherry from the cocktail stick.

"Are they all like this?" I asked.

"What?"

"Bars? Only, it's loud, isn't it?"

"We can go somewhere else after if you want. Somewhere more quiet. I thought we'd want to grab something to eat. Unless this whole thing's a fucking disaster, in which case we'll finish these and call it a day." He laughed.

I bought the next round, this time a bottle of overpriced European beer for me and another cocktail for Julian.

He took his drink from me. "What's with the outfit?"

"Don't you like it?" I gestured to the new on-trend jeans and bright shirt with pink and blue flowers across it.

"I almost bought this." He pinched the shirt between his thumb and finger. "I've got a pair like these." He pointed to my jeans.

"I just threw them on," I lied. "Found them in the back of my wardrobe." I avoided his eyes and checked the time on the wall clock. Still too early to suggest dinner and we were now talking about my clothes. Oh dear.

"Back of your wardrobe. Pull the other one. It's trendy. Look, it's what everyone's wearing." He gestured to the rest of the bar. "I'm not sure it's quite you, though. It's very smart, but I liked you in your old blue jeans and lumberjack shirts. They're you. You look comfortable in them. At the moment, you look like you're outside a headmaster's office waiting to be called in and bollocked."

"Thanks." I tucked the shirt into the jeans, wishing I'd picked something else to wear instead, and then wishing I'd not asked for Olive's help and had done it all differently—everything from coming out to her, to asking for her help and even writing to Julian. "Where's the gents'?"

"Far corner. But go in the ladies' if there's a queue. No one will care."

On the way in, I caught the eye of the topless barman who'd served me earlier. I hadn't been able to keep my eyes off his chest— all golden tanned and completely hairless. I wasn't used to getting a side order of erection with my drinks. Straight pubs don't have topless barmaids so why should there be topless barmen here?

He winked and smiled. As I passed the bar, he handed me a card. "Fancy staying around until I finish? Go for a coffee or something."

"I'm on a date." I shrugged my shoulders. "At least, I think I'm on a date."

"All right, mate, hope it goes well. If not, you've got my number."

I ran to the toilets and stared at myself in the mirror. *What a fraud I am. Who do I think I am, trying to fit in with all this lot at forty?* I was already past it, judging by how many other guys my age or older were there. A topless, smooth-chested barman and there was me wearing a floral shirt with the top button done up and a few stray hairs from my hairy chest poking from the collar.

Once I was back leaning against the wall next to Julian, I said, "I've got it all wrong. I'm not right. I'm sorry, but I think I'd best go."

"Hang on a minute." He stopped me leaving by grabbing my arms. "You were the one who begged me to give this a go. You were the one who said you wanted to have a relationship. You're the one who's been doing all the chasing. I'm here because I thought I'd give you the benefit of the doubt and give it a try with a relationship, and with someone who was pretty obviously very messed up."

"Thanks," I replied, staring at the floor.

"You are messed up. You told me you were. Did you think you'd come out here tonight and hey, presto! you'd be ready to be gay like the rest of us? You've spent your whole life living as a straight man. Of course there's gonna be some things you don't understand, things you don't want to do, things you feel you don't fit into. But you need to try them to at least work out what does work for you. To be honest, I did wonder if this was the right place for a first date, but then I asked some friends and they said it was as good as anywhere else. Next time, we can go to the cinema. Later, we can have dinner. I was going to suggest one of the gay restaurants on Old Compton Street, but maybe not."

"They have gay restaurants?"

"Love, they have gay removals companies, gay handymen companies—gay everything. If you want it."

I shook my head. "It's not just this place. It's everything. I don't know how to be when I'm with you."

"Be like you were before. You were lovely before. You were so lovely, in fact, that I'm breaking my *no relationships* and *no being strung along by a straight man* rules. Just for you."

"I am not a straight man." I stuck my bottom lip out.

"What's the problem?" He turned me around so I was facing him and held both my hands in his.

"How does it all work?" I couldn't think of anything else to say to explain what I meant.

"Just like with any relationship, I suppose—I'm basing it on relationships with friends because I'm no expert—you work it out as you go along."

"I don't know if you want me to be the one getting the drinks at the bar and paying for dinner, or if I'm meant to be that person? Or if we take it in turns. I don't know how to be with you anymore because all I'm thinking about is getting it right and wrong."

Julian pressed his index finger across my lips. "Shushhh. Stop worrying about all that and we'll go back to how we were before. Before we were trying to be anything, back to two guys who like each other and have a laugh together, and who happen to find each other attractive. How's that sound for starters?"

I nodded. Sounded simple enough when he put it like that.

"And just so's you don't feel left out, feel that.'" He put my hand on his chest over his heart. "That's me, shitting myself while I'm on my first ever date."

I laughed quietly and pulled myself closer to him so he was pressed against the wall, and I kissed him on the lips, lightly at first. His lips tasted of nothing, not lipstick or lip balm, just lips. Pressing harder, I felt his stubble against my face, so much rougher and harder than kissing a woman. I pushed my whole body up against his, so my hand was squashed between us, and felt something against my hip, pressing through Julian's jeans.

"Is that what I think it is?" I whispered into his ear.

"It's not a gun, so I must be pleased to see you," he replied before returning the kiss. This time, he bit my lips gently, sucking on my mouth, drawing out the air as our lips locked together. He pushed himself towards me and took my hand from resting on the wall behind him and placed it on his bulging jeans. Pulling back from the kiss, he said, "Never mind your clothes. That's how much *you* turn me on."

I looked to either side, expecting someone to tell us to move along, to calm down, to take things outside, but nothing.

"They don't mind. As long as we're keeping hands and cocks inside clothes, they don't give a shit."

"You want me to know how turned on you feel, don't you?" I breathed in the hot air between our mouths.

"Why wouldn't I?"

"None of this love me, respect me?"

He shrugged. "Men generally want sex. Even in a relationship, it's still about sex. As far as I've seen, anyway."

We stood like that for a while, pressed closely together, Julian's back to the wall and my body covering his.

After a while, he pushed himself forward and said, "Enjoying it?"

It was obvious I was enjoying it, just as much as he was, so I nodded quickly. This was the first time I'd enjoyed this feeling without letting the guilt overtake it—of being with a man, of being turned on by being with a man—and that was as much of a turn-on as being turned on itself.

"You said you wanted to leave. Still want to leave, or stay here?" he asked with a smile and a wink and a lick of his lips.

Because I wasn't hungry any longer and because I wanted to go to a place where I could touch him and be with him, I said, "Dancing. Can we go dancing somewhere?" So he knew the real reason I was suggesting this, I added, "Somewhere gay."

"Of course," he replied and took my hand, leading me out of the bar, down a few streets and into a club.

There, we drank little bottles of expensive European beer, and it tasted like the best honey I'd ever had. The dance floor was filled with men of all shapes and sizes, some wearing white T-shirts and jeans, some in black plastic shorts, and everything in between.

For the first few beers, we sat at the bar and Julian talked to the barman—topless and wearing only a pair of gold hot pants and gold sandals—while I watched and nodded in agreement at their conversation.

Eventually, the barman said to me, "Don't you talk or what?" I smiled, shrugged and stopped staring at his body.

The barman turned to Julian. "Is he foreign or something?"

"Just come out."

"I see." The barman popped up onto the counter, his feet on my side and hands extended behind him, lifting himself up so his straining legs and golden hot pants were inches from my face. "You like that, don't you? I've seen you staring at me all the time I've been talking to your friend. Well, get a good look. No shame. Take it all in. I'm all man, I like cock, and I'm proud of it."

Julian laughed and spat out a bit of beer as the barman thrust his groin in my face. Julian banged his hand on the bar. "Did I tell you how we met?"

The barman dropped back to the floor as gracefully as a cat jumping from a fence to the ground. "I've gotta hear this."

Over three beers—we bought the barman one for his performance—we told him about the Sallie concert and the giant glitter ball falling and hitting Julian.

The barman said it was the best story he'd heard, and if we stayed together it would be something to tell our families. With that, we left him serving another customer, juggling bottles and cocktail shakers and flexing his muscles in his gold hot pants behind the shiny bar.

On the dance floor, at first, we danced like I'd done with my friends as a teenager: opposite each other, staring over the other's shoulders with three feet separating us. Then, because I didn't know how to do it, Julian took my hands and we danced holding hands, moving closer until we were dancing with our bodies touching and the now familiar stiffness pressing into me. My head was swimming with the combination of the beers and the atmosphere, but I wasn't so drunk that I didn't know what I was doing.

I wanted to kiss this man—this man in his late twenties, or early thirties—who still refused to tell me his exact age. This man whose erection I could feel pressing into my hip as he grabbed my bum and pulled me an inch closer to him while all around us the music played and the others danced and the lights flashed. As he kissed me, I found myself wanting to kiss him back harder than he'd kissed me, to taste him on my tongue, to rub his stubbly cheek against mine. I pulled back from the kiss, rubbing his cheek against my neck. A shiver of electricity ran down my neck, down my chest and into my stomach. "Brush it against my face," I breathed into his ear, barely managing to get the words out. I wanted more of that feeling, whatever it was.

He kissed me quickly, softly on my lips, then turned his head so his cheek was brushing against mine, slowly moving from my left cheek to my right, then back under my chin and to my neck.

"I'm not hungry," I said breathlessly.

"Back to mine?" he suggested.

I nodded, rubbing his face against mine again and loving the bristly, burning sensation that was so new to me.

In the taxi, we kissed and rubbed and licked and bit, and I felt as if I was about to explode. He brushed his hand against my erection through my tight trousers, and before I could say anything, I gasped and shook and felt a wetness on my thigh. "I've... Too much..." was all I managed.

Julian laughed, staring at the damp patch on my jeans. "Fucking hell. I've never had that effect on a man before!"

The taxi driver's voice filled the rear of the vehicle in a tinny artificial tone. "No mess on the seats. Wait till you get home or I'll charge you a cleaning fee."

"It's all right, we're all done now!" Julian said, then laughed again.

"I'm so sorry." I wiped the patch on my jeans with a tissue I found in my pocket. "I'll get out here and see you whenever." I tapped the glass between us and the driver.

"What you doing?" Julian asked.

I shook my head. I had never felt so embarrassed in my life.

He told the driver not to stop, held my arm and said, "Jump in the shower at mine. I'll lend you some new clothes. No worries." He smiled.

I could hardly look him in the eyes. Mortification filled my body.

He pulled my face up so I had to meet his eyes. "We've all done it. When I was a teenager, admittedly, but it's come to us all." He laughed. "Sorry, couldn't resist."

"I couldn't stop. It was so... Nothing like I've ever felt before. I was..." I trailed off, aware of the taxi driver's flapping ears.

We didn't talk for the rest of the journey, just held hands in the back of the cab.

***

Julian introduced me to his flatmate, who was watching TV in her pyjamas with a shower cap on her head and a bowl of something strong and chemical smelling on the table in front of her. She held out her hand. "Angie. Glad you could finally join us in our boudoir."

I shook her hand. "I hope we're not interrupting. It wasn't planned. I said I should go home, but he wouldn't have any of it."

Julian disappeared for a moment then reappeared and threw me a towel. "Bathroom's through there. My bedroom's on the left. Help yourself to anything you can fit in."

I smiled weakly at Angie. "It's been a long day. Sweaty." I made a big show of sniffing my armpits and walked to the bathroom as the embarrassment of what had happened followed me like a bad smell.

I closed the door and heard laughter from the living room followed by a loud, "No way!" from Angie. *Bollocks. Is there anything he doesn't share with people?*

***

Clean and dressed, I joined them in the living room. Angie's hair was now ice blonde, and the bowl of chemicals had been replaced by a bowl of popcorn as they watched a film.

I sat with them on the sofa, Angie in between us. She grabbed our hands, joined them and said, yawning exaggeratedly, "I'm so tired. All this being a hairdresser has really taken it out of me. I think I'll go to bed and listen to some music." She left the room.

He moved closer to me on the sofa, and I shuffled across towards him until we were rubbing thighs together.

"She didn't have to do that. I feel bad, chucking her out of her own living room." I stared at her bedroom door from which some whale-song-type music escaped the bottom of the door.

"Don't mind her. She'll get all the gory details later." He winked.

"Will she? Does she have to? Really?" Knowing that made me feel uncomfortable. More uncomfortable than I already felt.

"OK, only edited highlights. Besides, when she first started going out with her boyfriend, it was like *Nine and a Half Weeks* every time he stayed. I used to go out in the end—couldn't stand the noise. He was a screamer and an *oh-yes*-er. Not pleasant. Wore thin in the end." He walked to the kitchen and opened two bottles of beer from the fridge then returned, handing one to me and sipping one himself.

My hands were shaking as I held the bottle.

He clinked our drinks together and steadied my hand, holding it gently in his. "What's up? I'm not going to bite. We won't do anything you don't want to. In fact, if you want, we can sit here and watch the rest of the film with the popcorn. You can sleep on the sofa tonight and I'll be in my room. Whatever you want."

That sounded comfortable, gentle, easier than what I'd been expecting. "Yeah. Let's do that." All I knew was I didn't want him to stick anything up my bum.

And so, we sat on the sofa, watching the rest of the film, eating popcorn and occasionally stopping to talk about it, and kiss, quiet kisses which sometimes built into a little bit more neck kissing and biting, but I quickly pulled back, worried of a repeat of what had happened before.

As the credits filled the screen, Julian collected the bottles and bowl we'd been using and tidy them up in the kitchen.

I took the plate over, then, not knowing where anything went, put it in the dishwasher and watched Julian go about his business. Every time he bent over to put something in the dishwasher or pack something away in a low-down cupboard, I found myself staring at his bum. His bum, encased in his jeans. When he reached to the higher cupboards to pack away glasses, I noticed the skin on the small of his back had a dusting of very light, soft-looking hairs.

He returned to the living room and pulled out the sofa bed, covered it in bedding and yawned, stretching his arms high above his head to reveal, I noticed, a tiny knot of dark brown hair around his belly button.

I felt myself instantly stiffen. Stiffen in a way I'd never done before with a woman, where, now I allowed myself to admit it, I'd always proceeded through the stages of foreplay to sex a bit like I was colouring in by numbers. Ever since reading an article in a woman's magazine about foreplay, I'd stuck to the sequence they advised and the techniques for the ultimate act itself. I'd had no complaints so far, and it gave me a useful list to tick off while I was doing it, to keep my mind on the job and ensure I appeared enthusiastic.

Now, I felt an arm around my shoulder and Julian was saying goodnight to me. He kissed me and pulled back to start walking to his room.

His smell and the taste of his slightly salty lips from the popcorn and the roughness of his face against mine all combined as I looked at the sad little pull-out bed and thought about Julian's queen-size bed in his room where I'd lay earlier, naked and just out of the shower. "Let's go for it," I said quietly.

He turned back to face me. "You what?"

"If you want to. Only, I think it's been long enough. I could give it a go again, this time I won't...you know."

"Come in your pants?" He smiled.

I laughed. "Try not to, anyway."

Without saying anything else, he turned the light off, grabbed my hand and led me to the bedroom. "It's not very comfortable, anyway. Piece-of-shit sofa bed." He closed the door.

***

You're probably disappointed I'm not telling you what we did, but I couldn't. I felt it was something between us two, and also to be honest, I'm not sure if I've got words for some of it. His years of being a filthy fucker had definitely done him good in the bedroom department. Never mind my sex-tips foreplay; this was foreplay, back play, front and sideways play. Anyway, afterwards, lying in bed together, I started to say something I'd turned over in my mind a few times before opening my mouth. "Thanks," was all that came out.

"No need to thank me. You were there too. You did your fair share. Once I showed you how, mind, but soon enough you were like an old pro."

I laughed.

"It's not like it's a new type of body for you, is it? I've not got anything you've not got. Now, women's bodies? A complete mystery to me. I was having a crisis of confidence, or an identity crisis, anyway. I said to Angie I didn't know *for sure* if I was straight or bi. If I'd not been hiding it all these years."

"Hiding it well." I smirked.

"All right. No need to take the piss. Anyway, she sat astride me, in her bra and panties, and put my hands on her breasts then asked me if I felt anything."

"And?" I raised my eyebrow, this would be interesting...

"Nothing. It would have been like trying to stick a jelly in a rabbit hole."

"Lovely image." I closed my eyes.

Sighing, he went on, "She jumped off me and said she was relieved otherwise it would change how she felt about me. I've always been Julian who's gay, since she first met me."

That was one of my biggest worries—how people would change what they thought of me when I told them I was gay. How in their mind I'd always been Troy. Nothing about being gay to it. "I didn't think I could feel like that with another person. I've not done before. Never mind another man. It was..." I struggled for the words to explain how I felt at that moment.

"Don't worry. I feel the same. Well, not the same, the same— it's more like a dawning of realisation. I think I've been so long fuck-and-go, I forgot there's another way to do it. Not another way. I mean, there's only so many different ways to do it." Julian turned to face me, resting his head on his arm. "I can't believe you're here." He looked me up and down.

"I am. Look."

"When I first met you, I didn't think we'd end up like this. I thought you'd be another man I'd think about, fantasise about being with, but who wouldn't be with me, 'cos you're...well you were, straight."

"Do men really do that to you?"

"What?" Julian asked.

"Pretend to be interested just to get you in bed and then leave?"

Slowly, deliberately he said, "All the time."

"Straight men? With you?"

"Back to their girlfriends and wives, all of them. Yep." He sighed and asked if I wanted to have a shower or fancied a drink.

I shook my head. I didn't want to leave where we were right now, right there, ever. I had everything I wanted all in one room. In one bed, next to me.

"Why St John Ambulance?" he asked while stroking my forearm.

"Why not?" I replied.

"I mean, why not work in the ambulance service for the NHS and get paid for it?"

"I do want to be a paramedic and work for the NHS."

"So why aren't you doing it? They'd pay you too, you know!"

"Too old." I sat up and stared straight ahead, avoiding his gaze.

"How old's too old?"

Shrugging, I said, "Too late, then. Couple of years training and I'll be early forties. What's the point?"

"Another thirty years of doing a job you enjoy, that's the point."

"How's the dancing?" I asked, wanting to change the subject as I knew I had a weak argument but couldn't be bothered to respond any further.

"How long would it take to train?" he asked, more persistent than I'd taken him for.

"The house is good, I enjoy gardening. Since when did you become a careers advisor?"

"I remember dancing in the living room at my birthday party. It was 'Japanese Boy' by Aneka—it's so camp, but I didn't know that then, of course. I was skipping about on the living room floor singing about how I missed my Japanese boy." He rolled his eyes.

"How old?" I frowned.

"Six. See, I'm doing what I always wanted to do, since I was a little boy. You should do what you want to do and not let age get in your way."

CHAPTER 18

Julian

W<small>E WERE AT</small> a bowling alley and I, contrary to my best wishes, was wearing a pair of the ugliest shoes I'd ever had the displeasure of seeing. "You've got to wear them," Troy had said.

"I'd rather swallow razor blades," I had replied.

"There's nowhere for you to do that, so you'd better get on with the shoes and the bowling, since we're at a bowling alley."

So here I was, staring at the rows of people in their hideous shoes and throwing the heavy silly balls down the long alley to hit the stupid white things at the far end, only for them to be replaced with a new row of white things to do the same again. It was sport light—the sort of sport where you didn't have to do much, could kind of rumble along with not much actual movement—my sort of sport, basically.

"Pick a ball," Troy demanded, pointing to the row of shiny coloured balls filling cages behind the alleys.

"How do I know which one to get? I've got big fingers, but I'm quite weak." I tried to pathetic up my response.

"Try a few, see which one's comfy."

Because I was feeling a bit bloody-minded, and thought it would liven things up a bit, I picked the bright pink ball. Holding it with both hands, I walked up to Troy and showed him. "Now what?" I asked.

He showed me which fingers to put in which holes, and how to hold the ball with two hands, then explained the swinging-arms-with-ball thing that was apparently required to get a good straight bowl and hit the white things at the end of the lane.

My first go went straight into the edge, missing all ten of the skittles—Troy explained that was what the white things at the end were called.

For my next go, he stood behind me, pulling my arm back as I held the ball, showing me how to do the special swing move he'd explained. I knocked two skittles over, and when I turned, clapping a little to myself, he was clapping too and said, "Well done. Only eight more to go."

Troy had the next go, and I watched him line up the ball with the skittles, swing his arm backwards... I missed the ball itself as I was focusing on the view of his arse as he bent forward and his jeans rode up slightly at the back, tightening around his arse cheeks—arse cheeks I wanted to dive in between at that moment.

The next round, I knocked five skittles down. Heady on a combination of Troy's arse cheeks and my own ability to half-do a sport, I jumped up and down, clapping and shouting, "Five! I did five this time. That's half, isn't it?"

"Tenpin bowling. Clue's in the name." He pointed to a bright purple ball. "Try that one. It's a bit heavier."

Enjoying the moment in the spotlight and the continued warm glow of the part success, I said, "But it's not as pretty as my ball. Can't I wait for mine to come through the thingummy?"

He shrugged.

I waited for my shiny pink ball to arrive but nothing happened.

Eventually, I picked up the purple one Troy had suggested and asked him to help me line it up.

He looked from one side to the other at the nearby bowlers, then strode up, stood behind me and showed me how to line up with the arrows on the lane to hit the five remaining skittles.

I followed his instruction, while he stood behind me, and knocked the five remaining skittles down. I jumped up and down and turned to face him. I wanted to kiss him. I wanted to hug him. I wanted to scream. I did scream. I shouted, "Strike, spare, whatever it is, I got 'em all down. I own this bowling lark!" Then, because I didn't think he'd want to kiss me there and then, I danced my little victory dance down the lane and back again, cheering to myself like I was a one-man cheerleader. I skipped a little as I arrived back to the seats where Troy sat. "Sorry." I knew I'd gone too far; too much too soon. I knew the others would be watching me and Troy would be mortified.

He wiped his hands on his thighs. "Don't be sorry. Don't ever be sorry for being you. All right?"

"All right?" I replied, sitting next to him.

He put my hand on his thigh. "It's taken me all this time to work out who I am, to be able to be who I am. Don't you go changing who you are. You are who you are, and that's why I want to be with you. You stay you. All right?"

I nodded.

We had reached the end of the frame, or the game, or the section, or something. Anyway, we needed to pay if we wanted to play some more. "Shall we get something to eat?" I asked.

"I could eat." Shrugging, Troy grabbed my hand, pulled me close to him and kissed me. A proper *snog in public lingering for a few seconds* kiss. Then, still holding hands, we walked to the burger bar.

CHAPTER 19

Julian

B JORN HAD INVITED me round to his place for a film night—
"To watch a film," he had joked. "And that's all."

This was a whole new stage of our friendship, and one I was keen to make work. I couldn't imagine not having him in my life after so long.

He opened the door of his flat in Chiswick and kissed my lips then cheek. At the same time, I handed him a bottle of wine. *Lips, cheeks, face, holding hands—what do we do now?* I wasn't sure, and I didn't think he was either.

He led me to the kitchen where he opened the wine and poured it into two glasses. Handing me one, he said, "This is for us. This is for us to carry on the film nights. Properly." He winked as we clinked glasses.

We talked for a while about what we'd been up to—him doing some serious partying after Sallie's UK tour and me being quite couply with Troy and finding it actually quite enjoyable. "It's like, I'm turning into my parents, but I don't care." I shrugged and waved the thought away dismissively.

We walked to the living room.

He said, "You do not have to do that. You are still young. Plenty of fun to still be had." He stared at the white plastic chair in his living room which I knew had a removable hole in the seat allowing people to sit in comfort while Bjorn did his party trick for hours on end.

I stared into my wine glass, not wanting to blush at the memory or let him know what I was remembering.

"Do you still stay tonight?"

I nodded. I wanted it to be as like before as possible. I'd explained this to him while we'd talked about what films we might watch.

"You do not really want the sofa bed, do you? I know you said, but I thought we would sleep in my bed. Like usual." He smiled then topped up my wine.

It was what we'd always done before. Only before, I hadn't had a boyfriend. "Sofa bed. Yes." I replied, concentrating on the chair but trying to see it only as a chair and not the scene of fun and filth and depravity courtesy of Bjorn.

"Do you not trust me?"

"I don't want to put myself in a situation where something could happen I'd regret." In all honesty, I didn't completely trust myself if I was sharing a bed with Bjorn and had a stomachful of wine. "If it's too much hassle, I'll just go home tonight."

He stood and disappeared to a cupboard, pulling out a pillow, duvet and sheets, huffing and puffing and saying he didn't mind, and whatever I wanted. He piled up the bedding beside the sofa. "Happy now?"

"Have you cooked?" I sniffed the air filled with spices and herbs.

"I have. I have used a recipe book."

***

The recipe book and Bjorn had done well. The chicken in sauce with rice and vegetables was delicious. The second bottle of wine was wonderful too. It went down much quicker than the first, which meant the third bottle didn't seem to touch the sides.

And that was how I found myself at the bottom of the bottle, sitting on the special plastic chair, with the cushion covering up the hole, as Bjorn lay on the white sheepskin rug, his head near me.

We had been laughing about something or other. It seemed hilarious at the time—something to do with a Sallie song, and changing the lyrics to be very rude—and then he'd told me about this guy he'd slept with who said he was only into the sex but afterwards had wanted to hug and then texted and messaged him three or four times an hour.

Good times. Just like old times, in fact.

He lay on his back, staring at the underneath of my chair. "What's he like?"

"Who?"

"Fireman man?"

"St John Ambulance, and he has a name—Troy. He's a gardener too."

"He is good with his hands. This, I like the sound of." He licked his lips and laughed to himself.

"He's great. He's funny, in his own quiet way, and he's fun too."

"Sounds like he has everything. I mean in bed, you silly. What is he like in bed?" He lowered his voice on the last two words.

"I'm sorry we've not seen much of each other lately. It's been busy with work, and then I took time off, and then you were off. But we're here now."

"We are." He removed his T-shirt, revealing his toned and trimmed-of-hair chest. "It is hot in here."

It was no hotter than usual. Certainly not hot enough to start stripping.

"Is he big. He is a tall man, no? They can be small, I find. How does he like it?"

I said nothing, wishing we could leave this particular juncture of conversation.

"He is straight. Is he good in bed, just tell me this."

"He thought he was straight. He's with me now."

"Does he know what he is doing? Have you showed him the ways?" He laughed and licked his lips. "Does he fuck you or do you fuck him? Some straight men, they like me to fuck because they say they enjoy not being in charge, being passive in bed. This, they like. What about your Troy?"

I stood and walked to the kitchen, carrying my wine glass.

He shouted, "What is wrong? What did I say wrong?"

I returned to the living room with a glass of water. "It's not the same as before. We can't talk about this stuff like it's just some random shag. I'm with him. It's different. Do you understand?"

He nodded slowly.

"I've hardly seen you at work. Where have you been?"

"Me, I had time off and wanted to be a good boy. No partying, no fucking, no drinking. Sometimes." He rolled onto his back and laughed to himself. "I missed it. I missed you." He pointed to the chair.

I sat in the chair.

He edged himself closer and removed his jeans. "You know what I like."

"We went to this restaurant, it was a converted church in the East End, run by two brothers. French, I think. It was almost a religious experience. The food was so tasty."

He said nothing, instead dressing slowly. Then he sat on the sofa on the opposite side of the room.

"I can't. I'd love to. But I can't."

He sipped his wine in silence. "I thought you wanted to come round because you wanted to *come round*. For our *film night*. And instead, all I hear is about you and Troy getting cosy together."

"You said it would be a proper film night."

"I say a lot of things. It does not mean that is the truth. You must know this about me."

This time, it was me who remained silent.

After a while, Bjorn broke the silence. "Me, I do not want to hear about your dates with Troy. It is boring, I think."

"Thanks. I know it's hardly salacious juicy gossip, but I thought you'd be interested."

"Maybe you would think this, but I find it not so interesting." He shrugged and turned his back towards me.

"I thought you'd be happy for me. You always said I should try a relationship, see how it goes, and now I have, and I'm happy."

"You, I think, have changed. I do not know who you are."

"It's still the same me." I touched his back, trying to turn him to face me.

He turned and looked me up and down, sizing me up. He shook his head. "I cannot be happy for you."

"Why not? Fuck's sake, we've got through worse shit than this. What's so bad with this that you're like this." I paused, staring into his eyes, trying to look for a faint glimmer of the old Bjorn cheeky smile.

He stared back at me, unsmiling. "I cannot be happy for you because I think you make a mistake."

"I wanted my friend's support and advice. That's why I came here, not to sit in your chair with you underneath. Is that so hard for you to understand?"

He folded his arms. "I understand well. But…" He bit his lip.

"There's something else. Tell me. Fuck's sake, we've seen each other naked hundreds of times. You probably know my body as well as I know it. You've seen me at my worst. Tell me."

"I thought I would be fine. But now, I realise I cannot go from what we had to this, listening to you talk about your boyfriend. I cannot do this change."

"Why not?" I had a good idea why, but I wanted him to say the words himself.

"Now you have gone. Now I do not have you, I know how I feel about you."

I said nothing.

"I fancy you. I have always felt like this, but now I know I want a relationship with you. Because I can't. What we had was almost a relationship, I think. We had friendship, and laughs, and the sex too. This, for some, is a relationship." He shrugged. "I want sex and friends with you, but only you."

I'd always thought we were both on the same page with our arrangement. We'd had many discussions about how well it had worked, for both of us, how mature we were to be friends one moment and in bed together the next, only to return back to friends again. It was only now that I realised this was because, during the whole time, I hadn't been in a relationship.

When Bjorn had briefly had boyfriends, it hadn't bothered me; sex and friendship were two separate things in my head. I got sex with others during those times and still had Bjorn's friendship. I had never thought of him like that before.

"I didn't know you felt that way. I thought we were all about being mature, and separating sex and love and friendship."

"Me too, I thought this." He avoided my eyes.

"Why are you telling me now, when I can't do anything about it?"

"I thought you knew. I thought it was obvious."

"Not for me, it wasn't." I put my hand on his knee, wanting desperately to get back to the comfortable intimacy we'd had for our whole friendship up to this point.

"I only knew this when I saw you with him."

"He has a name."

"I cannot be friends with you and watch you with Troy, hear about you with Troy."

I expected him to say more, to not have just left that statement hanging between us, so brief and so final, but he said no more. So I said all I could think of saying in response. "What sort of a choice is that? Don't make me choose."

"I have thought about this for a long time. This is the only way."

I removed my hand from his thigh, stood and walked to the door.

He shouted after me, "You can stay on the sofa if you want. We can talk more. I was stupid—the jokes about the special chair. You know I joke. Take no notice of me. "I can do this. I want to make this work, that's why I'm here." He was standing next to me now, by the door, leaning against the doorframe. "Me too. This is why I told you."

"My door is always open because I can have you in my life as only a friend. I want both you and him in my life."

He started to reply then closed his mouth, pursing his lips.

"Can you let me out please?" I asked.

He obliged, and I left his home, for the first time without staying the night, and for the first time without a hug and a kiss or a vague promise of when we'd see each other again. At that moment, I felt a deep sadness for something I'd lost and would probably never have back again.

CHAPTER 20

Troy

I WAS SITTING IN my clothes in the changing rooms as my teammates put on their football kits all around me.

Someone slapped my back. "Don't hang about, Troy mate. We're on in ten, and Coach wants to have one of his talks." It was Lee with his broad smile and twinkling brown eyes.

Not twinkling—who thinks of their friend's eyes as twinkling? They were just brown eyes; nothing more, nothing less. I searched the room for a cubicle where I could change. There was none. I either got on with it, as I had so many times before, or I needed to go home.

"Mate, what you playing at? Get changed." Lee stood next to me, already in his red-and-white football kit.

I noticed the shorts were quite tight, and there was definitely some kind of lumpage going on there. I quickly shook the thought from my mind. I turned away from him, took my jeans off and threw on my shorts. Confident I'd dismissed any thoughts about football shorts and bulges, I changed into the team top and turned back.

"Where you been for so long?" Lee asked. "Thought you'd dropped off the face of the earth or something."

"Needed some space." Like I needed some now. Coming back to play football so soon was a big mistake. What made me think, after being up close and personal with Julian, I could handle a sweaty changing room full of naked men and it wouldn't be a problem? What a twat. "Took a while to get over Freya, you know?" I threw in as if that would explain everything.

"Someone saw you. Said you looked well. I can't see it, as it goes. Not at the moment, anyway. Maybe you shouldn't be playing." He sniffed and rubbed his nose on his arm. "Someone heard you were getting on well at work."

"I was. I am." I'd arrived at football practice all chatty, asking the lads how they were and if they'd missed me, promising I was back on form, asking if they wanted a drink afterwards, so it made sense he would say that. Only I didn't feel anything like that anymore.

"Who's keeping you so happy now? Someone must be putting that smile on your face you had when you arrived."

I laughed and finished tying my boots. I was ready to play.

Lee said, "I always thought Freya was a keeper and you'd have had kids by now. Wondered why you hadn't, as it goes. And then bang, you've split up. Funny old world, innit?"

I started to form the words that would have led to me saying the reason I was so happy was someone called Julian, but before I could assemble the right words in the right order, Coach arrived, clapped his hands and started drawing our game plan on the blackboard.

***

I played better than I had before my break from football. I defended my boots off—one of the others said I was defending my arse off, but that made me think of Julian and I blushed, so I ignored that one. They carried me from the pitch to the changing room, pouring water on my head and throwing leftover slices of orange at me, telling me not to disappear again—"'Cos we thought you'd fucking gone and topped yourself," Lee said with a smile and a wink in that way people say things so serious with a dismissive air.

All considered, once I'd got changed into my kit, it had gone well overall, I suppose, but if I could have picked up my clothes and walked straight to my car without passing anyone, I would have done. Despite being covered in mud up both legs and my back from when I'd tackled someone, I was tempted to sneak past, but as I arrived in the changing room, I was met with a crowd of the lads half-dressed, squirting shower gel and shampoo at me. I caught a glimpse of someone's cock as he stepped out of the shower. Out of the corner of my eye, I noticed the smooth chiselled chest of another teammate. Already I felt myself responding in my shorts.

This could not happen. I looked either side of me for something to pull, an emergency exit cord, or an alarm of some description to take the attention away from me.

Nothing.

I'd been in this situation hundreds of times before with no problem. Because before I hadn't slept with Julian. Before, I'd spent my whole life pushing down any feelings about being attracted to men. Now I'd experienced how much I enjoyed sex with a man, and had seen how OK with it Julian was, being faced with a steaming shower of muddy sweaty men was like a living, breathing gay porn film. Full of my friends.

Shit.

I want to introduce you to my new partner, his name's Julian. There, that wasn't so hard, was it? Those were the words I needed to say, and then I could show them a picture of him on my phone—maybe one of the pair of us on a night out together in one of the gay bars he'd taken me to in London. Or, more likely, us sharing a packet of fish and chips from the day we went to Southend so I could show him the longest pier in the UK and he'd said, "The best thing about this pier is we're a mile and a half from Southend." With a cheeky smile and a wink, he'd kissed me, causing my heart to beat a bit faster and my hands to become a bit sweaty with excitement. I wanted to hold him close to me.

I stood by my clothes, eyeing up the shower as my teammates walked in naked and muddy and out naked and clean—a parade of variously shaped hairy and smooth bodies, all of which, ashamed as I was to admit it, I wanted to get a proper look at.

I leant forward, stripped off my shorts and pants, willing my semi-erection to disappear, then, as casually as I could manage, removed my top, throwing it on the floor, and walked to the shower, the towel still around my waist. Only when I was confident everything down there had returned to normal size did I drop the towel and step under a hard stream of water, turning it to cold so I didn't get too comfortable and nothing got too enlarged. I kept my eyes closed, only briefly opening them to squirt shower gel on my body, quickly rubbing it and then rinsing it off. Confident I'd rinsed off all dirt and gel I bent forward, picked up my towel from the damp floor and held it in front of me before wrapping it around my waist and running my hands through my wet hair.

I concentrated on dressing and staring only at my pile of clothes, despite being joined by others standing naked and dripping as they asked me about going for a drink. Finally, I walked to my car, blinking quickly to stop the tears—of concentration? Of frustration?—running down my cheeks. I panted and rested against the door.

Lee's voice woke me from my temporary dream. "You all right, mate?"

"Not used to running. Been too long without playing. My own stupid fault." I laughed, not even convincing myself never mind Lee.

"Something ain't right. Tell me. I'm your mate. You can tell me." He held the door as I tried to open it.

I shook my head, forced his arm out of the way and got in the car. "See you next week." I left the car park, wiping my eyes with my sleeve and wondering how the fuck I was meant to carry on as normal.

***

"See you soon." Julian winked as he waved at me through the window.

Perching on the windowsill, I watched him walk along the road with his bright-red backpack and then slumped back on the sofa, surveying the empty room. I wanted to go back to my room because I knew no one would see me there. No one would ask how I was, or if my friend had left, or any of those questions I knew would have me running to my room anyway.

A creak on the stairs signalled one of my housemates was coming down. It could have been anyone as the house's residents seemed to change on a weekly basis with rooms being emptied and filled with new people and their things.

I ducked out of the living room, into the hallway and up the stairs, crossing paths with my housemate without noticing who it was. Closing the door behind me, I caught my breath and leant against the wall. The duvet was pulled back and the sheets still showed signs of the fun we'd had half an hour before. The room smelt of salty, sweaty, manly, musky odours, and I inhaled deeply. This was my room where I could be myself without any worries about what others thought.

I sat on the bed and stared at the door. The door that led to the rest of the world where it wasn't quite so simple anymore. I noticed a pair of bright-pink designer briefs on the desk by the window. *Must have ended up there when he threw them.* I stared at the damp patch on the bed and instead of feeling warmth and joy and love for what we'd done—as I had at the time—I felt like a teenager whose parents had found his porn magazine stash.

I made the bed to cover the mess and then stood by the window. The pink briefs had looked so sexy on Julian earlier, clinging and bulging in all the right places. I'd removed them slowly so I could watch his face anticipating, allowing himself to break free and stick stiffly upwards. I had pulled them off with my teeth, and then I had made love to him with my mouth and tongue and lips until his back arched on the bed and he cried out for me to let him touch me. I'd undressed and lain on top of him, pressing my hot stiff cock next to his, still slicked from my mouth. We'd moved together, slipping and sliding, pushing things back in place to ensure the delicious friction of our bodies grew and built until we both finished in a stickiness that he'd wiped with the pink briefs and thrown them to the other side of the room.

Now, I picked up the briefs and retched at the memory. This was worse than being a teenager caught in his bedroom—this went much deeper—as deeply as the feeling in the woods with my friend on the camping trip. It was the same guilt hangover after the initial high of the act itself. *It is wrong and it is dirty to do those things with a man.* That was what I'd been brought up to believe, and even now, after coming out to some people, deep down, that was what I still thought.

What we'd done in the bed before had felt so right, and I had been able to completely let go, to completely give myself over to the moment, to the feelings, unlike any of the times I'd been with a woman. I'd always needed to concentrate on what I was doing, make sure I was enthusiastic enough, that I was doing it right, that I looked as if I was enjoying it. All those thoughts swirling around meant I usually didn't enjoy it much and it was more a case of getting through it, making sure she got what she needed, and then finishing with a smile plastered across my face. The tips from the magazine had been very useful.

I didn't need tips from a magazine anymore. I had Julian, and he'd been so kind and understanding and sensual every time we were together. It had been like learning to love all over again, only this time, to love properly.

So why, in my bedroom, now he'd left, did I feel like a dirty deviant who didn't deserve love or anything else I had with Julian?

***

A few days later, I was in the vegetable plot at work when Olive's voice woke me from a daze. I'd been thinking about the last kiss from Julian and how I'd thrown away his briefs the same afternoon because I couldn't stand to look at them.

"You got any veg in season, or is it all for show?" She peered down at the rows of neat holes I'd dug in the ground.

"Yes."

"And where are they?" She stared at me. "You were miles away. Anywhere nice? I could do with a holiday."

"Thinking about something. Last weekend." I smiled briefly at the memory of the afternoon in bed before he'd left.

"Wherever you were daydreaming, whatever you were thinking about, you seem much happier. And that's what counts." She smiled at me, raising her eyebrows in a way that said she wanted me to tell her more about why I was happier. I was used to this sort of look from people by now.

I sighed then picked up the spade and began digging more holes.

"Can't you tell me a little bit? I did help you with the first date."

I continued digging, concentrating on the spade and the ground and the weeds I was trying to remove.

"Bring whatever's in season and I'll make a soup or something. Best I leave you to it." Her footsteps faded into the distance.

I stopped digging and leant on the spade. "I can't tell you…"

Olive stopped in her tracks, head cocked to listen.

"'Cos I don't know how I feel. It changes."

She walked back to join me. "Say what you do feel, let's see how we get on with that."

"I'm happy when I'm in it, when I am it, with him. But when I think about it afterwards, I can't believe I am that person—a new person. And a new person I don't like much either." I wiped my hands on my jeans.

"You've got yourself in a right pickle, haven't you? All this thinking, it's not good for a person sometimes."

"Can't help it." I shrugged.

"Far as I'm concerned, you're still you—same person you was before, only now you're a bit happier, most of the time, anyway. Who says it's something to be ashamed of? If it's so shameful, how come they have these pride marches all the time? Now, tell me that."

I smiled at her logic.

"As long as you're not hurting anyone, and it's not illegal, what's to be ashamed of?"

I tilted my head from side to side to show I partly agreed and partly disagreed.

"Stop worrying what other people think. It's your life, live it." She pointed to the row of vegetables. "Bring me in some leeks and carrots, would you?" she said and then walked slowly back to the house.

CHAPTER 21

Troy

H E SAID IT would make him feel like a proper couple—"One of those ones you see in *Attitude* magazine, saying how they met and how they'd been together for years."

"What's it called, this gay restaurant?" I still didn't believe there was such a thing as a gay restaurant. And, how you could make a restaurant gay? But it seemed very important to Julian, so I agreed.

Julian asked the waiter, "Can we have one Tropical Love Land and a Blue Lagoon? And what are the specials?"

The waiter—too-tight black trousers and a very tight white shirt, a short ginger Action Man like beard and blue eyes—told us the specials and then stood waiting with his arms crossed. Julian stared straight back, winked and said we'd think about it.

Once the waiter had left, I knew I had to say something about the weird feeling Julian's response had given me. "What was that?" I flicked my eyes towards ginger Action Man in the far corner of the restaurant.

"Dunno what you're on about."

"The staring, blinking, winking, asking lots of unnecessary questions…"

"You've gotta admit, his accent's pretty sexy. Like a young Sean Connery. Smoking."

"Hadn't noticed." I had, but that wasn't the point. I had also imagined what he would look like holding a gun and driving an Aston Martin sports car, and surprisingly enough, they'd fitted him well. Suited him nicely, in fact. But I didn't tell Julian that or it would have weakened my argument.

"He can see my secret papers any day." Julian laughed and started pointing to the items in the menu he'd been thinking about choosing.

"That doesn't mean anything."

"What?"

"Secret papers."

"Oh, you know what I mean."

I looked around the restaurant at the bank of similarly dressed waiters and tables of mainly pairs of men sitting opposite one another, talking and eating. In the background, an instrumental version of one of Sallie's songs played, followed by another, this time with her high and slightly reedy voice included. "I see now."

"Steak and chips. What about you?" Julian didn't look up from his menu.

"Same. I said, I see now," I repeated myself.

"What do you see? To be fair, I think if you walked out of the sea in a pair of teeny-tiny little swimming shorts, you'd beat the waiter hands down. Gingers, pale skin you see. He'd not be good in the sun. Whereas you—" he gestured two hands at me "—Mediterranean colouring."

It had been a thought running around my mind off and on since we'd started dating, and his little performance with ginger Action Man brought it to the front of my mind. "Do you miss all the sex?"

"All what sex?" He frowned.

"With others. Since you've been with me, you've missed out, I suppose."

"Not from where I've been standing, or sitting, or lying." He smiled.

"What's with all the performance with the waiter?" Freya or Claire or any of the other girlfriends I'd had would never have done that so blatantly with me there, so why did he think it was OK? I didn't want to put it to him like that, bring it back to the difference between a relationship with a woman and one with a man, especially since we'd discussed it quite a few times before—badly and well—but now, I knew, was not the time for that particular argument. Instead, I said, "Seemed a bit weird."

"Have you ever been out with a big group of gay guys—at a restaurant or anything?"

"You know the answer to that." I paused for a moment, remembering the night club with the dancers after the girl band gig. That was a while ago. "There was this one time, in a club, but I wasn't right in the head. It didn't work. They were lovely. Helpful, friendly—it was me who needed to sort his shit out."

"So that's a no."

I shook my head. "It's a no."

"I've been off work for a bit, sitting around the flat with nothing to do, and I suppose I missed that bit. Not the whole thing, going right through with the full shag, but the first stages of it."

Our starters arrived with the ginger waiter doing his best to get Julian's attention and failing because he was now in the middle of talking to me. Eventually, after asking if we wanted anything else, the waiter left.

Julian continued, "I miss the beginning bit. The part where you're chasing someone, not sure if it's going to work or fail." He paused, filling his fork with smoked salmon and chewing it slowly. "It's like fishing, I suppose. Hunting, at least. Gets the heart rate up a bit."

"And that's all that was earlier?" I wasn't convinced, but given there was no other explanation coming from him, I thought I had to accept it. I turned to my starter and quickly dug in.

We ate in silence for a few moments and then he said, "If anyone should be worrying, it's me. Don't panic."

I'd finished my starter so put my cutlery down carefully although I really wanted to throw it on the table. Why was he the one who should be worrying? It was me who'd changed who I was for him, and my whole lifestyle. All he'd done was stop doing something—something that, when he'd told me about it sounded like he was pretty bored of it anyway.

"Right," I replied quietly.

"Because I've known men like you who've been all 'oh yes, I'm definitely gay', and then next time you see them they're back with their wives. It's a big step going from sleeping with a man to having a relationship with one. Much more—gay—if that makes sense. More than all the sex and all the kissing altogether."

"That's what you've done too."

"Have I?" He frowned briefly.

"Think about it. How many dates like this had you gone on before?"

"None. Because I didn't date."

"Exactly. So, looks to me like we're both in the same boat."

The waiter arrived with our main courses, and an awkward silence descended over the table.

Julian said, "I'd not thought about it like that before. You're right. I'm shit scared. And I bet you're shit scared too. So let's call the whole thing off!" He was waving his arms around like always when he was getting worked up about something.

"I don't want that. Unless you do." I paused, fork held in mid-air near my mouth.

"It's from a song. Or a play. Or something. Whatever, it doesn't matter—it was a joke. Christ on a bike, I need to get back to work. I'm all over the place without having it as an outlet."

"The St John Ambulance people called, asked if I wanted to do any more shifts. I keep saying no."

"Same here. And it's been easier to avoid Bjorn for a while too."

"Nothing from him?"

Julian shook his head.

"Still, it's been a good few weeks, hasn't it?"

"Twenty-two days, to be precise. I had a call, asking where I was, if I was still alive or had I dropped off the face of the earth."

"Bjorn?" I asked, hoping it would be and also hoping it wouldn't be from what I'd heard about him.

"Told you, nothing from him. No, this was Sallie. Wanted me to fill in for one of her new dancers who she realised was shit.

Said she knew I was on holiday and needed a rest, but would I do this one small favour for her?"

"Should've done it. Sallie asks, Sallie gets, I'd have thought."

"Usually yes, but she knew why I was taking a break. She remembered the incident on stage, with the glitter ball and the hunky man in the green jumpsuit. I said I needed some me time with my man. She understood."

"You should do it to help her out. How much harm is a couple of nights going to do?"

"I am getting itchy. I sang in the shower this morning. And while I was getting dressed. And making breakfast."

"I remember. 'Total Eclipse Of The Heart' is still running on a loop in my ears. I can see why you're a dancer not a singer." I smirked to myself, hoping he'd take the joke well.

Without missing a beat, he replied, "Sing like nobody's listening, dance like nobody's watching—I never really understood the point of that. Suppose that's why I do it on stage. Why would you dance and no one be able to see it?"

I'd heard this phrase before. It had been on a framed picture on the wall in my and Freya's living room. She often used to refer me to it when I was worrying too much about what other people thought.

"Love like you've never been hurt," I finished the rest of what the picture had said.

Julian nodded, blinking quickly. "Really?"

"Yeah," I explained about the picture. "That's what it said."

"Right."

We sat in silence for a few moments until our staring at each other was broken by the waiter's arrival and a discussion about desserts.

***

Back at my room in the shared house, I sat on the sofa in the corner. Julian had thrown...a throw—I believe it was called— over the top. The red furry cushion he'd bought sat on my bed. Although I hadn't gone with him to buy this...stuff—I couldn't think of another word for it—every time I looked at the cushion or sat on the sofa, they made me smile and think of Julian.

As he pranced into the room, I felt a warm rush of something for him, something like affection, I supposed. He certainly made me smile whenever I saw him—his little teasing jokes, his habit of bringing new colourful, unnecessary things to the house on his every visit. All these things. I patted the sofa next to me and he joined me. I said, "You know I love you, don't you?"

He smiled. "I thought I did, but now you've said it—as a question all the same—I'm sure now."

It was the first time I'd said the L-word first in a relationship since…forever, now I thought about it. "You brighten my life so much."

"That's better than asking me if I know you love me. You're improving. Like a wine with age."

"Thanks." And then we walked to my bedroom where I chucked aside the three mirrored pillows with green tassels—Julian had convinced me they were essential to the ambience of the room—and threw back the aquamarine duvet cover—not green, I'd been told—and we lay together on the bed.

***

Afterwards, we were in the kitchen making something to eat, dancing to a pop song on the radio. I closed my eyes and moved my arms and legs—what I thought was in time with the music.

Julian laughed and joined me, dancing next to me in the middle of the kitchen floor. "Good job you don't rely on this for money or you'd be homeless."

"Fuck off!" I shouted, still dancing, still enjoying how the music was taking me on a journey, much like how the man in front of me had taken me on a journey. "I enjoy it, so there," I replied, sticking my tongue out at him. "Dance like nobody's watching."

"And you're sure doing that," he replied.

We danced in the kitchen to the songs on the radio, while the pasta boiled and the onion stayed whole on the work surface.

CHAPTER 22

Julian

I ARRIVED HOME FROM a few days at Troy's place—the pasta was pretty soggy in the end, but the dancing and the kissing in the kitchen had made it worthwhile—and slumped on the sofa. My head ached from all the thoughts filling it on the journey home. I thought back to scenes from the previous two days—feeding each other in the restaurant; dancing in the kitchen; taking me to meet some of the staff where he worked… From where I sat on the sofa now, alone, it all looked like a boyfriend to me, and I didn't do boyfriends.

Before I disappeared into a black hole of my own worry and doubt, Angie arrived home, wheeled suitcase behind her and a bag of duty-free in her other hand.

Taking one look at me curled up on the sofa, she said, "He's not dumped you, has he? Decided he's straight again? Gone back to the other side? Don't tell me he fancies me?"

"Worse." I held my brow and closed my eyes, the headache surging through my skull.

"What?" Angie was sitting next to me on the sofa now.

"He said he loved me. L-O-V-E. I don't do love. Fuck knows what I'm meant to do with that now. What do you do when someone chucks an L-bomb into the room?"

"Rejoice? Celebrate? Say it back to him? These are all off the top of my head. What did *you* say?" she asked.

"I said 'yes, me too'. But I'm shitting myself. What if it all goes wrong? Then what?"

"Based on past experience, I'm guessing you get over it and meet someone else. You can't think that sort of thing while you're with someone or it's bound to jinx it." She had brought us a drink each—something orange, sweet and strong with a straw. "Get that down you and tell me what's going on in your mad little head."

"I feel like I'm stuck in this in-between place. I can't go back to fuck-and-go, because now I've had this, it would feel wrong. Actually, maybe I could go back to fuck-and-go, but I don't think I want to. But I can't stay where I am 'cos that scares me shitless too. Because next it'll be meet the parents, and moving in together and then marriage, and before I know it, I've turned into my parents. I'm not ready to turn into them yet."

"Dump him." She sucked the green glacé cherry off the cocktail stick.

"I will. Tomorrow."

"Do it now. Give him a call and tell him you can't be that person." She picked up my phone from the coffee table and handed it to me.

I took it and put it next to me on the sofa. "Tomorrow."

"How's the sex?"

"Fantastic. Magnificent. Breathtaking. Sometimes filthy. Sometimes tender." I could have said an awful lot more—and had done before with other men I'd shagged—but somehow, with Troy, I didn't want to go into details to Angie.

"All right for some. Do you fancy him?"

I'd had other fuck buddies over the years who, despite being amazing in bed and putting in a hard-working, enthusiastic performance, I'd have only wanted to see out of the bedroom if the lights were dimmed. I remembered once saying the fuck buddy had a face from *Crimewatch* and a cock like a baby's arm holding an orange, and given the two what was I expected to do? Now, I said, "I want to lick his face."

"I don't know what to tell you. I can't see a problem here." She lifted a cushion up on the sofa, then another, and then stood to look behind the door, moved into the kitchen and opened the cupboards one by one and eventually returned to the living room. "I can't find any problem. Except in here." She tapped my head. And that was how we left it. Angie, always one to be up for talking to death any issues or gossip on that night had reached the limits of her knowledge. And to a certain extent, so had I.

CHAPTER 23

Troy

I WAS HALFWAY THROUGH mowing the lawns at work and had been whistling 'Oh, What A Beautiful Mornin' over and over, particularly the chorus. With the sun shining on my face, the smell of freshly cut grass and the sound of birds in the trees, it really was beautiful, although when I checked my watch, it was well past morning—nearly two o'clock. I'd been mowing for almost three hours, without a break, and only the whistling to keep me company.

Olive walked across the middle of the lawn I'd half-mowed. She was waving her arms. I switched off the mower and waited for her to arrive.

"Fancy something to eat? You've been out here all morning without stopping for water or nothing."

I rested my legs on the steering wheel of the mower, a wide smile across my face.

"I take it the haircut and the waistcoat worked?"

I hadn't told her much since the first date with Julian. I hadn't wanted to be one of those people who talks about nothing but their partner. All bloody day. I also found it hard to get used to saying the b-word—boyfriend. Partner always sounded a bit formal, like someone who worked in a solicitor's firm or something. I tried out the word when I was alone, but with other people it sometimes got stuck in my throat.

I wanted to talk to people about him, mention it in passing, but when it came to saying 'boyfriend' to the woman at the post office or the man at the village shop when they asked how I was and why I was smiling so much, it hadn't quite come out right. I'd ended up saying 'b…rother'.

Now, I said, "Yeah. Suppose it did."

"I want to hear all about it."

***

We'd almost finished lunch before I built the courage to tell her about the big mistake I'd made—the one that had almost ended in us splitting up.

"We were in this pub, right, and we'd been sitting together, no problems. Talking, holding hands, not much. Anyway, this guy comes over and shouts abuse at him. Not me. It was like I wasn't there. This bloke watched as Julian went to the toilet, walked past the pool table and then shouted, '*Oi you, fucking queer.*' I couldn't believe it. I mean, I had to say something. I couldn't let him talk to someone I love like that. If it had been Freya, I'd have punched his lights out. Done."

"But would someone have said that about Freya?"

"No, but that's not the point. Someone I'm with doesn't need to put up with shit like that."

"That's what I'd have said too," Olive replied.

"Only not with Julian." Very much not indeed, as it had turned out.

"Why not?" Olive frowned and sipped her tea.

"He thought I was patronising him. Coming to his rescue and looking after him when he's used to dealing with that sort of crap on his own—for years before he met me, he said."

"Still, all's well that ends well."

"Yeah," I agreed. "It was funny meeting his friends, knowing he'd slept with them. When I used to meet Freya's ex, I always wanted to punch him, or not look him in the eye. Or both. But with this lot—his lot—his friends, I mean—they sleep with each other, then stop and carry on being friends. It's a whole new world."

"Sounds it. Fancy something for pudding?" She opened the fridge to show me a variety of desserts she'd made for the house which had been partly used and returned to the kitchen. I pointed at something that looked comforting and fattening.

"People stare at two men holding hands. People don't do that with a man and a woman. I hadn't realised before." I paused, thinking on the journey that had brought me to that point. "What a waste of forty years."

"Enough of this. It's the right time for you. Besides, it's better now than never. Imagine that."

"Julian said it's normal for gay guys to stay in touch with their exes—or ex-shags. I don't see any of my ex-girlfriends."

"Shopping? Has he taken you shopping?"

I shook my head. "Still hate it. Same with interior decorating, or musical theatre. I walked out of *Miss Saigon*. It was basically *Pretty Woman* with music. They can take her and I won't miss her." I paused. "I still don't understand it all."

Olive was stood next to me now. "Maybe you're not meant to understand. Maybe you're just meant to go with it."

"And his taste in music. Terrible. All the bloody same. I said I liked Sallie because it's his job and she's his favourite singer. But really, she's gone very far on very little, as the old saying goes. Mind you, having said all that, I am in love with a man. In a relationship with a man. I still am."

"Sounds pretty simple to me." She smiled.

"It is, and it isn't." I explained to her the difference between the twinks and the bears and the Muscle Marys and the metrosexuals and the spornosexuals. "Julian said, when he was younger, you could tell straight off who was gay and who was straight. Now the gays look straight and the straights look gay."

"Sounds complicated."

"Not really. Not once you get the hang of it." I rubbed my chin in thought. "That Carley…I've not seen her here for a while. What happened to her?"

"Left. Got herself a job in a supermarket. Said cooking wasn't her thing."

"Right."

"She told me to say goodbye to you. Said she understood why you did what you did. Said no worries about it."

"I was a bit of an arsehole to her, wasn't I?"

"If you'd have slept with her and then dumped her, then you'd be an arsehole. What you did, it was just confusion. You needed to sort your own head out. Best you didn't get her involved."

I liked Olive's logic, so I didn't argue with it. Instead, we sat in silence for a while until she asked if I could bring Julian to meet her, since she was practically there in spirit on the first date, and, "I want to see if he's going to be a heartbreaker."

"It's like having another mum," I replied, blinking quickly to prevent any tears rolling down my face.

CHAPTER 24

Troy

I HAD SOMETHING TO tell Julian. I wanted to be honest with him—I'd spent long enough telling lies to myself and the people I loved.

In a café near his flat, I saw him through the window, sitting in a low leather sofa and staring at his phone.

I hadn't wanted to meet at his place. Based on previous form, I knew what would end up happening, and although it would definitely be fun, I didn't want him to distract me from telling the truth.

We kissed briefly and I sat next to him on the sofa. He'd bought me my favourite coffee. I took a sip, imagining it had given me some sort of caffeine-induced Dutch courage and said, "I want to be honest with you. I can't carry on with the lies. They eat me up inside, after all these years."

He nodded and sipped his drink. He was playing with the silver ring on his right hand, twisting it around.

"You know Freya, my ex?" I wanted to start at the beginning. He nodded, still twisting the ring around his finger.

"I went for a drink with her and missed her. I wanted to give her something I'd taken when I moved out. But really, I wanted to see her. And when I was there, I felt like I had when we first met. I wanted to touch her, to kiss her, to love her." I shook my head.

Julian adjusted himself on the sofa and crossed his legs again.

"I'm sorry." I put my head in my hands. "I'm confused. I wanted to be honest with you."

"I can see this. You've spent your whole life being with women, and bang! Along I come and turn you gay. You're bound to have the odd relapse. As long as you're only looking but not touching." He smiled at me.

I coughed, assembling the words in my head in the right order. I'd been planning how to say the next part for days, wondering if it was better to come straight out with it or to pretend it hadn't been as bad as it really was, or to lie completely. After a long time, I had come to the conclusion I should be honest, not base my relationship with Julian on a lie. I chewed the inside of my mouth briefly. "I slept with her."

"You did what?"

"I was drunk. She was drunk. We were both drunk. It didn't mean anything. But I slept with her."

"You fucked her?" He stared at me, his eyes narrow and unsmiling.

"If you want to get technical, I had sex with her, yes."

"You put your cock inside her. You fucked her? Or was it just a bit of a wank, or some fingers? Or maybe a bit of a blow job and something for her too? Tell me. I want to get a good idea of what was involved, except the wine, of course."

"You don't want the details."

"Now you're telling me what I want?" Shaking his head, he pursed his lips and went on, "I don't think so."

I told him about the bottle of wine and the second bottle of wine, and the cuddle that had led to the kiss, and then how she felt so familiar and soft and comfortable, and how she'd unzipped my flies and grabbed me, and from that point onwards I'd felt powerless to stop, because one thing led to another, and the next thing I was lying on the sofa and she was astride me, enjoying me, and I was enjoying her, and it had all seemed so comfortable and easy, and how could anything that felt that good be wrong?

He listened, not saying anything in return until I finished, when he said, "Is that everything?"

I nodded.

"Fate's been having a good laugh at us two." He smiled the sort of smile I imagined a snake would before it pounced on a mouse.

"I'm so sorry. It meant nothing. Absolutely nothing. I can hardly remember it. The last bit I remember was the wine and the sofa, and then we were together. I don't know how it happened, but it did. She was on me. I was…in her, and it was…" I put my head in my hands and closed my eyes. After a while, I said, "I don't know how it happened." I waited for him to respond.

He stared at me, chewing his cheek slowly and tapping his foot on the ground. After a few moments of silence, he seemed to compose himself and sniffed loudly. "Suppose it evens itself up, then."

"What do you mean?"

"Tit for tat and all that. Makes it much easier what I was going to tell you, anyway." Swallowing, he blinked quickly—were those tears I could see? After a deep breath, he said, "While you were fucking your ex, I slept with Bjorn."

"Your friend Bjorn?" He'd mentioned him before, said they had some sort of arrangement when they'd both been single and that it had stopped since he started seeing me. "When was this?" I frowned.

"Last night." Taking a breath, Julian went on, "It's only sex. It meant nothing." He turned away and looked at me from the corner of his eyes. "Drunk. Wine was involved, obviously. We didn't fuck, but we still had sex. Or is it still sex if we didn't fuck? What do you reckon? I sucked his cock and then he sucked mine, and then we wanked each other off until we came. Is that sex? I mean, there was no penetration like with you and Freya. What do you reckon?" He stared at me, deadpan.

I didn't know what to say. This wasn't how I'd expected this confession to go.

"I knew I should never have trusted a straight man. Knew it would all come back to what you knew best. I was only ever a little experiment, I suppose. It never worked before, so why should it work this time?" He shrugged.

"Bjorn? You and him?"

Nodding, he said, "Yeah. And honestly, who was I, thinking I could settle down with one man forever? Ridiculous."

My stomach tightened, and I ran to the toilet where I crouched over the bowl and was violently sick. My forehead sweated, and my mouth tasted of acrid vomit. I had expected to apologise, to promise him it would never happen again, because really I felt I'd not been myself when it had happened, and then it would all be pretty much back to normal. This, I hadn't expected. This whole Bjorn and Julian thing, I had definitely not planned on that happening.

I returned to our table but sat opposite Julian. "I'm sorry."

"You said that." He was staring at his phone, very relaxed.

"Are you?" I asked, watching him and wishing we were talking about anything but what we were talking about at that moment. He didn't sound sorry.

"'Course I am." He threw it into the air like it was a nothing comment about having mayonnaise with his chips or wanting milk in his coffee.

"I'm confused. I am sorry. I didn't mean to hurt you. I want…" I wasn't sure what I wanted. At the time, with Freya, it had been fun, but now, sitting opposite Julian, I definitely felt much more for him. "I don't know who I want."

"Neither do I, it seems." He folded his arms.

"She's the only one—the only one time. What about you?"

"Anyone else except Bjorn?"

"Yeah."

His eyes narrowed as he stared at me. "I am easy. I never pretended to be anything else."

"So?" The tension was killing me. I had to know what other secrets he'd been keeping from me and how much of our relationship we could salvage from the burning wreckage left of it.

"I'm as pure as the driven sludge. Mae West said that."

"And are you?" I wanted to hug and punch him at the same time. I resisted both and instead stuck my hands in my pockets, my fists bunched and arms shaking slightly.

"As the driven sludge." He paused, licking his lips—lips I'd kissed so many times and wanted to kiss until a few moments ago. "All along. Ever since the start. A leopard never changes its spots and a slapper never changes her knickers. Well, I've not changed mine. Why should I have done, when you were still the same as before, still looking out for a nice woman, still thinking about your ex?"

I didn't know how to respond to that, so I said nothing. I wanted to reach out and hold his hands but at the same time felt repulsed by him, by what he'd done to me, to us, to himself. "Why wait until now to tell me?"

"I was waiting until you confessed. I could tell."

After a few moments, for wont of anything more clever to say, I said, "Fuck it."

"No, thanks."

We weren't getting anywhere. Why was he taking such relish in telling me he'd done as bad or worse as I'd done? Why wasn't he more angry with me for what I'd done? "I'm going."

"Leave me, I always knew you would," he replied, waving me towards the door. "Go on, the door's that way."

Standing, I put my hand on his as it rested on the table. "Neither of us can make up our minds what we want. All we're doing is hurting each other, so I think it's best to finish."

He nodded and squeezed my hand above his. "Fine with me." He stared out the window.

"You'd better not have given me anything from your sleeping around."

"My sleeping around? Pot—" he pointed at me "—meet kettle—" pointing to himself. He pulled me down to his level, talking quietly, directly into my mouth, inches from my face. "I'm a slag, and darling, I do it so well, and I love it. I am the Concorde of slags, but I'm also not a fucking idiot. I'm a careful slag—like Concorde, without the—" he coughed "—without the crash. Understand?"

I could smell the scent he almost always wore. Ralph Lauren, the one in the green bottle—I wasn't sure what it was called, but that was the bottle he had in his bathroom—and the same familiar smell I always recognised when he walked into the room.

CHAPTER 25

Troy

A FEW WEEKS LATER, I was at the post office avoiding telling the woman behind the counter when she'd next see Julian. We'd bumped into her at the village shop a month or so ago, when he'd been staying at mine for the weekend and we were stocking up on bottles of wine for dinner.

"Who's this young man?" she'd asked, staring at Julian in all his flamboyant glory.

"This, is my boyfriend, Julian," I'd said without a pause for thought and put my arm around his shoulder.

Julian had talked to her about a show he'd been watching on TV, and they'd bonded over the male lead. She'd said if she was twenty years younger she'd have been all over it.

Julian laughed and said, "Never mind that. Get stuck in now, I say."

And then, before I could say anything, he was telling her we'd see her later in the village pub so he could get to meet some of the others. Suffice it to say, he changed it from a normal Saturday night in a village pub to an impromptu karaoke night with spot prizes—donated by the post office, it seemed, after he promised to teach the post mistress how to dance to some of her favourite Sallie songs—and a speed-dating, getting-to-know-you part too—more drinking than tasting if I'm honest, but it involved everyone swapping tables and having to tell the others two surprising things about themselves. As was to be expected, after a few drinks, the whole evening descended into howling laughter from most people, even the shy ones.

Now, I was in mid-flow, talking to the postmistress about when we could perhaps repeat that, not wanting to tell her I'd split up with Julian, and as I said goodbye and I'd let her know when Julian was up for the weekend again, who did I bump into, but Freya.

"Sorry," she said, avoiding my eyes and tucking her blonde hair behind her right ear.

"Sorry," I replied instinctively. "What are you...I mean, why are you here? This isn't your local post office, is it?"

"Collecting something for someone." She smiled awkwardly and waved a piece of paper at me.

"Best let you get on," I replied, keen to leave the awkward situation.

As I turned to leave, she stopped me, grabbing my arm.

"Got five minutes, once I'm done here?" She bit her lip.

My gut said to leave, but something in her eyes said to stay. While she collected the parcel and talked to the postmistress, I shuffled my feet by the stationery and debated buying a diary for next year since I'd somehow got out of the habit of writing to Dave.

"Shall we go somewhere more private?" Freya asked, flicking a look to the postmistress.

***

In her car, we sat next to each other. It felt familiar yet strangely unfamiliar as I'd just received a text from Julian asking me how I was.

Freya said, "I need to say sorry."

"It was me who wasted your time for five years." That had been playing on my mind for a while, and I'd wanted to tell her how I really felt. I had to tell Freya it wasn't her fault we split up; it was me, and I felt guilty for wasting her time with someone who could never give her the things she wanted. She never thought me being gay was an option, but she was supportive because I was honest with her so she didn't blame herself for us splitting up. She didn't say much when I told her.

"Not that. I tricked you. I was hurt. I wanted to hurt you and your boyfriend." She said the boyfriend word softly, unlike how she'd said it before. "I heard you were seeing someone—a man—and I wanted to lash out at you both."

"I see." It didn't seem much like typical Freya behaviour, but I guessed she'd felt pushed into a corner by the whole sorry mess, so really, how could I blame her?

"It wasn't clever. It wasn't me. I still loved you and couldn't stand to think about you with someone else. The fact it was a man kind of made it better." She shrugged and, without my asking, went on, "Like he was giving you something I couldn't have given you even if I'd wanted. Like, it wasn't my fault."

I hadn't thought about it like that before. "I'm sorry. I never meant to hurt you. I thought it best to leave so you could find someone who could give you what you wanted."

Avoiding my eyes, she said, "And for you to find someone to give you that too." She coughed. "A different thing that you wanted. You know what I mean."

I did, and so I nodded.

"I don't love you, not like that, not anymore. But I still care about you. That's why I wanted to apologise. That's why I've been hanging about here waiting for you to come into the post office."

"Stalking me." I laughed quietly.

"If you want, yes." She laughed too. "I wanted you to be happy and wanted to put right what I'd done. My trick. I hope it didn't affect your relationship with your boyfriend."

Understatement of the century, but I didn't want to bother her with it so just said, "Long story, but it's OK now."

"I took advantage. I got you drunk and knew it wouldn't take much. You're very suggestible when you're drunk. I remember the happy laughing drunken sex after two bottles of wine we used to have on a Saturday night." She got a faraway look in her eyes.

I smiled briefly, remembering that too. "Are you with anyone?" Freya deserved to find someone to make her happy.

"Steve. Met him through work. I think I may be pregnant."

"That's quick!"

"I've known him for years. Always felt a spark but never did anything about it. He's moved in and things just rolled on from there." She rubbed her stomach.

"A lot of rolling on."

"I'm thirty-six, I don't have much time. He's kind. He's fun. He wants children." She stared at me, blinking slowly.

"I'm pleased for you. You're happy, are you?" I didn't know what else to say, so that seemed the best option.

"It's what I want. It's what he wants. Like I said, it sort of rolled on."

Again with the rolling on. I didn't blame her, not really, not after me wasting five years of her life and still not fully committing to her, or us, or building a family together. I stared at her stomach and imagined the tiny jelly-bean-sized baby growing inside her. A tiny jelly bean that could have been mine if so many things had been different. My stomach twisted slightly. "I'm happy for you."

"You said that." She paused, hooking her hair behind her ears. "Do you think we can be friends? Only, it's a small place, we're bound to bump into each other. I'd rather be friends than enemies. And the time we had together, it wasn't all bad. Not like the ending, anyway. We had fun, didn't we? We had good times?"

"We did. If you can get over me being gay then I can forgive you for trying to get me back through using wine and taking advantage of me. Most men would be grateful for a woman like you taking advantage of them."

"You're not most men." She placed my hand on her stomach. "I know you don't want children, but I think you'd make a good dad. I've always said you would. How would you feel about being an uncle?"

"All the glamour and none of the hard work, and I can hand baby back when I'm done?" I smiled. "I reckon I could get used to that."

CHAPTER 26

Julian

I WASN'T SURE WHY I'd lied about sleeping with Bjorn. I mean, it wasn't as if I'd even had the fun to go with the argument. That may have made it worthwhile. When I heard him talking about fucking his ex-girlfriend, I had felt so sick and as if he'd punched me in the stomach—the type of punch when you can't breathe and feel as if you're going to throw up everything you've ever eaten. It was as if the world was turning round to me and saying 'See? I told you so. This is what you thought he'd do, and look, he's gone and done it. Ha-ha, stupid idiot, thinking he'd give up a lifetime of women to be with you, what were you thinking?' It was what I had deserved really.

I was on my way to an audition for some background acting work; Sallie wasn't touring for another few months and the rent still had to be paid. As I left home, staring at my phone as I walked, I bumped into someone.

I knew it was him without looking. His musky smell mixed with CK One—a scent I'd told him had gone out with the ark, but he'd insisted he liked it and wanted to carry on using it—hit me.

I looked up from my phone. "I've got an appointment. What do you want?" *And why are you bothering to talk to me after my twenty-four-carat-gold fuck-off?*

He grabbed my shoulders and stopped me walking. "I want to apologise. I've been shitty without you. I've missed you. This can't be it. This can't be the end, can it?"

I removed his hands from me and continued walking, checking my watch.

"It wasn't a proper shag. It was just a hand job. She told me she tried to ride me, but I was too pissed to do it. So we had a bit of a fiddle instead. Hardly counts, does it?"

"Why'd she lie to you?" The irony of the question wasn't lost on me, but I wanted to hear his answer before considering whether I'd come clean with my confession. "Keep talking."

"I'm not me without you. I don't know how to be me without you now. You've helped me become this new person—a nicer person—and without you... I'm not who I was before, but I'm not him either. I'm..." He struggled to continue, clicking his fingers, trying to summon the words. "I'm someone who gets wanked off by his ex. I don't want to be that person."

"I lied." I figured, go in quick and soon, get it over and done with. He'd either forgive me, or end it. Either way, I'd know where I stood.

"About what?" He frowned.

"Said I'd cheated on you when you told me you'd cheated on me."

"Right. Is that normal behaviour in a relationship?"

"Fuck knows." I licked my lips, took a deep breath and continued, "I was hurt when you told me. It was what I'd thought would happen ever since we got together, my biggest fear. You don't get all this hurt and exposure with a fuck buddy. It's simple—in and out, and go away. I'd never felt like I did when you told me you'd cheated on me. Felt like you'd stuck your hand in and ripped out my insides. I wanted to hurt you as much as you'd hurt me. So I made it up."

"What did you make up?"

"Me and Bjorn—all of it. We saw each other, and yes, he tried it on, gently, but I left. I couldn't cheat on you. I chose you over Bjorn."

"Nothing happened between you two?" He stared at me, furrowing his brow and narrowing his eyes.

"Nothing. Not since we've been together, anyway. A kiss was as far as it went. Just one kiss."

"So it was only me who fucked up out of the two of us?"

"If you want to look at it like that, yes. I don't think it's that simple, really. We both had a wobble—it's all new to both of us, in different ways. You don't do relationships with men, and neither do I. And here we are, both trying to have a relationship with a man." I laughed to myself, the irony of how similar our situations were finally dawning on me.

"One thing I do know." He held my hand, stroking it gently. "I was really miserable without you. And no amount of thinking about Freya or any other woman made up for that. It was you I wanted. You I wanted to kiss, to hold, to be with, to love. You." He shrugged. "I keep saying I don't know who I am, but actually I've realised I do. I'm this person, the person who loves you, who wants to be with you."

"I never thought a man like you would say that to me before. Never. All the dirty fantasies I talked to Bjorn about, and this is where I end up." I laughed quietly to myself.

"It's not a joke. It's gonna take me a while to get used to being this person, the man who's not straight, who is gay. I always used to see gay guys, you know, the really obvious ones, the flamboyant ones—"

"Like me?" I couldn't resist adding that in, with a smile and a wink.

"Yeah, like you, and most of your friends. I saw you and thought how brave you were."

I touched his lips to silence him. "Listen, sweetheart, I don't need any of your pity. None of us lot do. So don't think this is a pity party."

"That's not what I mean. It's taken me this long, my whole life, to work out I can be gay in this way. A big butch football-playing man, can be gay too. But the more flamboyant gays, you're the ones who are much more men than me, much more brave."

"How so?" I wanted to hear where this argument was going, wanted to give him the benefit of the doubt.

"Because you're out there, in the world, not sticking to what the world says a man should be. You're true to yourself. Not like me, hiding for all these years. Wasn't it the drag queens who started the Stonewall riots?"

"Some say so." I raised my eyes in recognition of his gay history knowledge. "I'm impressed."

"Same in every way. It's harder for men like you to be who you are in public. I've heard what people shout at you, the looks people give when you say you're a backing dancer for Sallie. But you're just being yourself. And you don't let anyone tell you how."

"Suppose so. Hadn't thought of it like that before. I just sort of get on with it. Take the bullying and abuse—whatever they throw at me—and throw glitter right back at them."

"It's true. I've been thinking about it ever since I met you. I can't live as miserably as before, pretending to be someone I'm not, and so I'm living my life as you do. I'm getting used to the awkwardness, because it's easier than the black deep sadness I had before." He blinked slowly as a tear rolled down his stubbly cheek.

I wiped it off with my thumb then kissed him. "Well, you've got me now, so you'd better get used to that too."

***

I walked off stage as the crowd cheered Sallie's finale song— one of her old classics from the eighties, a cover of a pop song from the sixties with a fake drum track, synthesisers layered throughout and a chorus and dance moves mimicking a train that everyone knew by heart.

I caught my breath, took a sip from a bottle of water a friend handed me and suddenly Sallie appeared backstage. Her red glittery dress billowed at the base and pinched into an almost physically impossibly thin waist, revealing deep cleavage I was tempted to drop my phone into. "Come with me." She held my hand.

"Everything all right?"

"It will be." Her ace-of-hearts hat wobbled as she walked quickly to a small room with 'first aid' written on the door.

"I'm fine. Just a bit of water, I'll be great. Honestly, I'll get changed and see you in the bar in a bit."

Sallie shook her head and touched my lips to silence me. "Not yet, you won't." She opened the door to a small room with an empty single bed and a chair.

On the chair sat Bjorn, wearing jeans and a tight-fitting white polo shirt that showed off his biceps and chest to their best advantage.

I turned to Sallie. "I don't think this is right. I didn't ask to meet him. We're not—"

"And that's why you're here. First aid for your relationship. I can't stand it when people fight. You two. Sort it out." She winked at Bjorn, gave him a quick flash of her crossed fingers, then shut the door.

After a few moments, I said, "How's things?"

"Things are shit. You?" Bjorn tapped his hands on his thighs.

"Me and Troy are back together. It wasn't—" I stopped myself, remembering how Bjorn had said he wasn't interested in hearing about my relationship, how it made him feel. "Fine."

"What happened?" He swallowed loudly. His Adam's apple bobbed up and down his throat covered in three-day stubble. "This, I want to hear."

I told him about Troy's confession and Freya's trick, and how I'd lied about what Bjorn and I had done—or hadn't done—to lash out at Troy.

Bjorn blinked slowly after I'd finished. "I am sorry."

"Me too. We both said stuff. Cruel things. Nobody died. No harm done, I suppose."

"There was, I think. Harm to us. Julian, I missed you. I do not think we have spent this long apart since we met. I did not know what it would be like. I was childish. I am sorry."

"I missed you too." It was only now, as he sat feet away from me, I realised how much I had missed him. "Can I hug you?"

He nodded quickly.

We hugged, his familiar smell—the scent he always wore and the hair product he always used—swept me back to the night of the argument. I blinked away a tear that appeared for some reason.

"I should be happy for you, and not jealous of you. I missed us together. I missed our friendship. I needed this more than I needed to not hear about you and Troy." He hung his head and shook it.

"It's all right. We'll work it out."

"We must be able to work it out, how to be friends again without the extras, now you're with Troy. I want to work this out. It was only sex."

"That was the idea," I replied.

"I feel stupid because I told you how I felt, and you do not feel the same. This is harder than seeing each other naked, I think. This is harder than being dumped by someone, because, you— you are still in my life, and we know what I said, and what you did not say. This is the worst."

"Can we just take this angst down a notch, please? You said you fancied me. I didn't say anything. You know I fancy you, otherwise why would we have slept together so often?"

"Because it is just sex?" He shrugged. "Because we both like a lot of sex?"

"Maybe, but we had the friendship too. That made it easier to do the sex because we knew what each other wanted. Look, we could talk about this all night, but I'm with Troy now, and he wasn't too keen on me carrying on with our film nights. It is possible to *not* have sex with someone, you know. We're not animals."

"Yes, this I know."

"How many other men have you slept with and carried on seeing as friends?"

"Many," he replied quietly.

"Or we wouldn't have many friends, right?"

"Right."

"So this is no different. I've seen your cock, you've seen mine. I'm with Troy, you're free to be with whoever you like. Let's not call the whole thing off."

"Sorry," he said again. "I do not know what has come over me before."

"Me a few times if I remember rightly!" I laughed.

"This is true," he said. Looking up at me, he went on, "I'm happy for you. I really am. But I am sad that we're not messing around with each other anymore."

"Doesn't mean we can't be friends and still have our film nights, but without the happy ending." I smirked.

For weeks, he'd not spoken to me at work, not returned my calls or emails—nothing. Once, he'd broken the wall of silence and said he preferred it if we weren't anything anymore. Not friends, not lovers, nothing. That had really hurt. More than I imagined it would. It made me realise how much of a good friend he was and how much I would miss him if we stopped being friends.

Now, he was laughing, rocking back on his chair, slapping his hands on his thighs at a particularly dirty question he'd just asked me about Troy compared with him in bed.

I shook my head. "A lady doesn't tell."

"Fuck me, you really have changed!" He slapped his thighs again.

"He's nothing like I'd have imagined him being—my perfect boyfriend. Nothing like Troy."

"Really?" Bjorn raised an eyebrow.

"Emotionally. Spiritually. All those -ally things people go on about when they meet their partner for life."

"Boring, is he?" Bjorn smirked.

"No. Quiet. He didn't know what to say to Angie when he first met her. Sat there like a muted mullet until we got a few drinks into him."

"When will I meet this perfect specimen of manhood?"

"I wouldn't go that far. He can be pretty frustrating sometimes. But—" I shrugged like it was nothing "—I suppose I don't mind."

"Because you love him?"

I shrugged again, shaking my head, trying to play this down as much as possible. "Suppose I do." Taking his hands now, I said, "I love you too. Only it's different."

"And me too, I think," Bjorn replied in his typical deadpan way.

Sallie opened the door to check we were OK. "You boys kissed and made up?" she asked.

"We have," Bjorn replied.

"We're all down in the bar. Come down before the tab runs out." In a whirl of red sequins and swish of manmade fibres, she was gone.

CHAPTER 27

Julian

I DECIDED TO TAKE a break from the dancing and touring with Sallie and the others. I found myself wanting to be in London more and away much less. Bjorn kept me filled in with the gossip when he came round for film nights—strictly only films and pizza. My agent had managed to get me some music video work—standing behind a row of girls who hadn't made the grade individually on a talent show, but when put together had somehow managed to become the next Bananarama/Girls Aloud/The Supremes, depending on your decade of reference.

Basically, it had been an easy day's work. I'd learned the moves easily and got on with the other two male dancers; one wanted to get into stadium-tour dancing, so I'd told him about Sallie, and the other was a straight guy who had wanted to do stripping but his girlfriend wouldn't let him, so dancing was a good compromise. It hardly felt like work, really, posing for some photos, standing behind the girls singing their harmonies, repeating the same seven moves again and again and occasionally glancing into the camera.

I called my agent—to tell him how it had gone and ask if he could get me some more similar gigs—on the way to the bar around the corner from the recording studio.

Bjorn greeted me, hugging me and kissing both cheeks. "You're here. I heard. The long-lost wanderer returns." Pausing, he said, as if he'd been rehearsing it for some time, "He has travelled to a planet we only know as Boyfriend, and we gather here to hear his tales."

Rob, one of my friends from a few photoshoots ago—designer underwear in bright colours on a beach in the Canaries—shouted my name and arrived with a tray of shots. "How's it going with settling down?"

"Loving it." I smiled at him and took a shot from the tray as he offered it.

"Bjorn says you and he used to be more than friends. And you were known for playing the field. And there was me, thinking you'd been with Troy for years and years."

Bjorn shouted, "He's a gardener. Has he told you that?"

Rob shook his head, downed another shot, then said, "Do I need to make the joke? Or is it too obvious?"

Everyone in chorus shouted, "Uphill gardener? Too obvious."

Troy arrived at the door, head and shoulders above most other people, scoping around to find us. I waved, and he strode over, kissing me and hugging me, then staring at the group of us.

Everyone in the group looked him up and down.

"All right, lads?" Troy asked.

Rob, having never met him before, was all over him, hanging on his arm and stroking his back, offering him a shot from the seemingly endlessly filled tray of bright liquid.

Without any objection or hesitation, Troy downed one shot and then another, wiping his mouth on the back of his hand. "Now what?"

Before long, we had finished the tray of shots and were on our second bottle of cava. Rob sat on Troy's lap and I sat next to them. I wasn't bothered at all about that, but what did piss me off was when Troy started to ask about the worst things I'd done during tours with Bjorn and the others.

Highlights included, but weren't limited to—"He ran off stage to throw up in a fire bucket because he was so hungover from the night before. We kept it from Sallie because the show had to go on, and she'd warned him once more and he'd be out."

I denied this, of course. "She wouldn't have been worried. She knows she couldn't manage without me."

Bjorn replied, "Take no notice. If I had not done anything, he would have gone." After much laughing at my expense, he said, "We'd been invited into the celebrity bar afterparty by Sallie. Sometimes she does this if it's been a really good concert. Sometimes it's her and her celebrity friends and we make do in the hotel bar. He—"

"I have a name," I spat.

"Julian—he was at the bar doing tequila shots with that radio DJ who used to present breakfast TV twenty years ago, and the woman who's all about crafting up your house—really posh accent, does that property programme. They were hammered. Posh presenter woman's laying her head on the bar, face resting in a pool of liqueur, and the radio DJ is striding along the bar."

Bjorn was enjoying this now. I could tell by the sly smile and sideways glance he gave me before he started his next story. "He went missing for a whole day once."

Troy shook his head and looked at me.

"All day. We arrived in Seville, I think it was, did the show, and went clubbing. He disappeared. We thought he had been kidnapped. Twenty-four hours, only just long enough to not be able to contact the police. But sure enough, he turned up with no trousers or shoes."

Bristling slightly at this affront to my personality, even though it was true, I replied, "I had my shoes, but I had lost my socks and trousers."

Troy said, "Well, that's all right, then." He laughed to himself, putting his arm around my shoulder before kissing my cheek.

CHAPTER 28

Julian

A FEW MONTHS LATER, I was on stage getting ready for Sallie's final closing number. It was the biggest single from her latest album—about meeting someone who was so wonderful they didn't compare to all her previous lovers. It was one of my favourites of her modern songs.

I took my position and prepared for the cue of the opening bars. While dancing, the screen behind the stage showed line drawings of male and female bodies together in various combinations with hearts between them. It was a simple message and a song I loved.

As Sallie sang the final words, the audience cheered, still waving their hands and cigarette lighters in the air from the last chorus of singing together. Sallie said, "I'd like to dedicate this song to one of my loyal—I don't do favourites—male dancers, who's worked with me for the last five years. Julian. Can we have some applause for Julian?"

The audience cheered.

Sallie motioned to the edge of the stage, and Troy walked on to join her.

I had no idea what the hell Troy was doing there.

He took my hand and knelt on one knee. Sallie held the microphone to his lips, and Troy said, "I have wasted enough time. I love you and don't want to waste any more time."

My stomach was doing somersaults and my throat was dry, my hands sweaty. We'd casually talked about marriage, but only in a *wouldn't it be nice some day in the future* way. He'd told me so many times he had never felt like this with any woman he'd been with and now knew what it was to properly love someone. But this? This was definitely a surprise, and much sooner than I'd thought it would happen. Who marries their first boyfriend, really?

Now, Troy said, "Will you do me the honour of being my husband?"

I realised that none of the previous lovers I'd had compared to Troy, not just in the bedroom, but in the way he was with me when we were together—the little things he did for me, and the things I did in return for him, not because I felt I had to, but because I wanted to—and I knew I could say only one thing.

"Yes. Yes I will."

Sallie stood between us and said into the microphone, "Looks like I'm buying a new outfit."

The audience cheered, and Sallie started singing the opening lines of the same song with the audience joining in.

***

A few weeks later, Bjorn was round my place, asking me how plans for the wedding were progressing.

I told him some details and then, as the enormity of the situation hit me, said, "I wanted a loving, sexual relationship, and I never thought I could have both in one person."

"Because you hadn't tried to have both in one person before."

Well, that about summed it up, didn't it? "No," I said.

CHAPTER 29

Troy

I HAD SPENT SO long being afraid of who I really was that it became second nature to me. Men like Julian used to scare me—so proud and loud and so gay—how could they be like that in public, and not be ashamed? Getting to know him, realising I was attracted to him, and eventually loving him, I realised that was what I'd needed to be the real man I should have been years before. And seeing Julian, so proud, unashamed, and living his life in screaming colour, made me see he was as much of a real man as any other.

I feel comfortable as me, just me as I am, for the first time since I was a child, since before I had been told it was different and it was dirty and it was wrong. Now I've told people, I can breathe properly, I can let go, be who I really am.

I'm all types of macho—how was I meant to be gay like that?

I couldn't be gay—I wasn't how gay men were.

I'd tricked myself that my feelings meant nothing, that I was looking at the clothes not the men. I was miserable, burying the feelings. I wasn't miserable with Freya; she was a loving, caring, girlfriend—everything I could have wanted in a partner—except she wasn't the gender I found attractive.

We had a long engagement to give Julian time to plan the wedding. And when I say plan, I really mean plan—venue, flowers, outfits, music, food—everything.

Sallie performed—unplugged. Instead of the big honeymoon she offered to pay for, Julian said he'd like her to perform. She wanted to give us both away, but even Julian felt that was too much.

We had a joint stag do, because, why not? And we invited both male and female friends—some of my old friends from my football team and the house mixed with Julian's dancing friends and clubbing friends from London. My favourite picture from the night was a line of everyone starting with Bjorn and including my football friends, Olive from work and Julian's friend Angie, arms around each other in a colourful messy crowd, just like in life.

The ceremony had thirty close friends in the grounds of my work and ended with a party for 150 that evening with Sallie singing.

As she finished her set at the wedding, she said, "Julian, the man who was always looking for the next man to climb..." The crowd laughed at that before she continued, "I'm so happy you've found Troy. And Troy, just remember it's never too late to be who you want to be. I know Julian and you will love each other for the rest of your lives." She proposed a toast to us then, before dancing to the cheesy music disco with our guests.

None of these things were anything I would have believed would happen to me, or anyone I knew, but sometimes life doesn't turn out as you imagine. Sometimes life throws things up for you that take you on a journey you never believed you'd take.

The End

ABOUT THE AUTHOR

Liam Livings lives where East London ends and becomes Essex. He shares his house with his boyfriend and cat. He enjoys baking, cooking, classic cars and socialising with friends. He has a sweet tooth for food and entertainment: loving to escape from real life with a romantic book; enjoying a good cry at a sad, funny and camp film; and listening to musical cheesy pop from the eighties to now. He tirelessly watches an awful lot of *Gilmore Girls* in the name of writing 'research'.

Published since 2013 by a number of British and American presses, his gay romance and gay fiction focuses on friendships, British humour and romance with plenty of sparkle. He's a member of the Romantic Novelists' Association, and the Chartered Institute of Marketing. With a Master's in creative writing from Kingston University, he teaches writing workshops with his partner in sarcasm and humour, Virginia Heath as https://www.realpeoplewritebooks.com and has also ghostwritten a client's five-star reviewed autobiography.

Social Media

Website: http://www.liamlivings.com

Facebook: http://www.facebook.com/liam.livings

Twitter: https://twitter.com/LiamLivings

Blog: http://www.liamlivings.com/blog

BY THE AUTHOR

For Liam's other stories check out his website
www.liamlivings.com

BEATEN TRACK PUBLISHING

For more titles from Beaten Track Publishing,
please visit our website:

http://www.beatentrackpublishing.com

Thanks for reading!

Lightning Source UK Ltd.
Milton Keynes UK
UKHW04f0017130918
328795UK00001B/28/P